CITY OF FEAR

(An Ava Gold Mystery—Book Two)

BLAKE PIERCE

Blake Pierce

Blake Pierce is the USA Today bestselling author of the RILEY PAGE mystery series, which includes seventeen books. Blake Pierce is also the author of the MACKENZIE WHITE mystery series, comprising fourteen books; of the AVERY BLACK mystery series, comprising six books; of the KERI LOCKE mystery series, comprising five books; of the MAKING OF RILEY PAIGE mystery series, comprising six books; of the KATE WISE mystery series, comprising seven books; of the CHLOE FINE psychological suspense mystery, comprising six books; of the JESSE HUNT psychological suspense thriller series, comprising nineteen books; of the AU PAIR psychological suspense thriller series, comprising three books; of the ZOE PRIME mystery series, comprising six books; of the ADELE SHARP mystery series, comprising thirteen books, of the EUROPEAN VOYAGE cozy mystery series, comprising four books; of the new LAURA FROST FBI suspense thriller, comprising six books (and counting); of the new ELLA DARK FBI suspense thriller, comprising nine books (and counting); of the A YEAR IN EUROPE cozy mystery series, comprising nine books, of the AVA GOLD mystery series, comprising six books (and counting); and of the RACHEL GIFT mystery series, comprising six books (and counting).

An avid reader and lifelong fan of the mystery and thriller genres, Blake loves to hear from you, so please feel free to visit www.blakepierceauthor.com to learn more and stay in touch.

ALREADY TRAPPED (Book #3)
ALREADY MISSING (Book #4)
ALREADY DEAD (Book #5)
ALREADY TAKEN (Book #6)

EUROPEAN VOYAGE COZY MYSTERY SERIES
MURDER (AND BAKLAVA) (Book #1)
DEATH (AND APPLE STRUDEL) (Book #2)
CRIME (AND LAGER) (Book #3)
MISFORTUNE (AND GOUDA) (Book #4)
CALAMITY (AND A DANISH) (Book #5)
MAYHEM (AND HERRING) (Book #6)

ADELE SHARP MYSTERY SERIES
LEFT TO DIE (Book #1)
LEFT TO RUN (Book #2)
LEFT TO HIDE (Book #3)
LEFT TO KILL (Book #4)
LEFT TO MURDER (Book #5)
LEFT TO ENVY (Book #6)
LEFT TO LAPSE (Book #7)
LEFT TO VANISH (Book #8)
LEFT TO HUNT (Book #9)
LEFT TO FEAR (Book #10)
LEFT TO PREY (Book #11)
LEFT TO LURE (Book #12)
LEFT TO CRAVE (Book #13)

THE AU PAIR SERIES
ALMOST GONE (Book#1)
ALMOST LOST (Book #2)
ALMOST DEAD (Book #3)

ZOE PRIME MYSTERY SERIES
FACE OF DEATH (Book#1)
FACE OF MURDER (Book #2)
FACE OF FEAR (Book #3)
FACE OF MADNESS (Book #4)
FACE OF FURY (Book #5)
FACE OF DARKNESS (Book #6)

A JESSIE HUNT PSYCHOLOGICAL SUSPENSE SERIES
THE PERFECT WIFE (Book #1)
THE PERFECT BLOCK (Book #2)
THE PERFECT HOUSE (Book #3)
THE PERFECT SMILE (Book #4)
THE PERFECT LIE (Book #5)
THE PERFECT LOOK (Book #6)
THE PERFECT AFFAIR (Book #7)
THE PERFECT ALIBI (Book #8)
THE PERFECT NEIGHBOR (Book #9)
THE PERFECT DISGUISE (Book #10)
THE PERFECT SECRET (Book #11)
THE PERFECT FAÇADE (Book #12)
THE PERFECT IMPRESSION (Book #13)
THE PERFECT DECEIT (Book #14)
THE PERFECT MISTRESS (Book #15)
THE PERFECT IMAGE (Book #16)
THE PERFECT VEIL (Book #17)
THE PERFECT INDISCRETION (Book #18)
THE PERFECT RUMOR (Book #19)

CHLOE FINE PSYCHOLOGICAL SUSPENSE SERIES
NEXT DOOR (Book #1)
A NEIGHBOR'S LIE (Book #2)
CUL DE SAC (Book #3)
SILENT NEIGHBOR (Book #4)
HOMECOMING (Book #5)
TINTED WINDOWS (Book #6)

KATE WISE MYSTERY SERIES
IF SHE KNEW (Book #1)
IF SHE SAW (Book #2)
IF SHE RAN (Book #3)
IF SHE HID (Book #4)
IF SHE FLED (Book #5)
IF SHE FEARED (Book #6)
IF SHE HEARD (Book #7)

THE MAKING OF RILEY PAIGE SERIES

WATCHING (Book #1)
WAITING (Book #2)
LURING (Book #3)
TAKING (Book #4)
STALKING (Book #5)
KILLING (Book #6)

RILEY PAIGE MYSTERY SERIES
ONCE GONE (Book #1)
ONCE TAKEN (Book #2)
ONCE CRAVED (Book #3)
ONCE LURED (Book #4)
ONCE HUNTED (Book #5)
ONCE PINED (Book #6)
ONCE FORSAKEN (Book #7)
ONCE COLD (Book #8)
ONCE STALKED (Book #9)
ONCE LOST (Book #10)
ONCE BURIED (Book #11)
ONCE BOUND (Book #12)
ONCE TRAPPED (Book #13)
ONCE DORMANT (Book #14)
ONCE SHUNNED (Book #15)
ONCE MISSED (Book #16)
ONCE CHOSEN (Book #17)

MACKENZIE WHITE MYSTERY SERIES
BEFORE HE KILLS (Book #1)
BEFORE HE SEES (Book #2)
BEFORE HE COVETS (Book #3)
BEFORE HE TAKES (Book #4)
BEFORE HE NEEDS (Book #5)
BEFORE HE FEELS (Book #6)
BEFORE HE SINS (Book #7)
BEFORE HE HUNTS (Book #8)
BEFORE HE PREYS (Book #9)
BEFORE HE LONGS (Book #10)
BEFORE HE LAPSES (Book #11)
BEFORE HE ENVIES (Book #12)
BEFORE HE STALKS (Book #13)

BEFORE HE HARMS (Book #14)

AVERY BLACK MYSTERY SERIES
CAUSE TO KILL (Book #1)
CAUSE TO RUN (Book #2)
CAUSE TO HIDE (Book #3)
CAUSE TO FEAR (Book #4)
CAUSE TO SAVE (Book #5)
CAUSE TO DREAD (Book #6)

KERI LOCKE MYSTERY SERIES
A TRACE OF DEATH (Book #1)
A TRACE OF MURDER (Book #2)
A TRACE OF VICE (Book #3)
A TRACE OF CRIME (Book #4)
A TRACE OF HOPE (Book #5)

PROLOGUE

Evelyn Johnson knew she had a good paying job, so she felt ungrateful when she belly-ached and fussed about the people she worked with. As an African American woman living in New York, she was very aware that her upbringing in this country sixty years ago would have been very different. Her mother had told her tales of how their people had been treated, particularly on the plantations down south. Compared to those horror stories, Evelyn figured she had been blessed by the Good Lord above and should just swallow down the little gripes she had about her job.

It was hard sometimes, though. She worked for a gentleman named George Pickett, a man that had been born into money, seemed to make more of it out of thin air, and spent it as if it meant nothing at all. Evelyn worked as a maid and cleaning lady for George and his prudish wife in their far-too-upscale Fifth Avenue house. And today was one of those days when George and Millie Pickett were getting rid of money like it was poison.

Today was their daughter's sixteenth birthday. And rather than give the girl a simple gift or a cake of some kind, there was something else going on—something Evelyn did not understand and, if she was being honest, made her quite angry. She'd heard Millie refer to it as a coming-out party. Some hoity-toity way to let all the other rich white folks in New York city know that their daughter, Penny, was now a proper young lady. Because apparently the ages of one-to-fifteen were just practice for being dolled over and made a fuss about when you turned sixteen.

The amount of money and attention going into this party was staggering to Evelyn. Millie had gone out to get a new rug and new curtains for the sitting room. Meanwhile, George had ordered cigars from some special place in France and they'd arrived on a boat several days ago. He'd been fawning over those boxes of smokes as if they were another child. There were all kinds of food being delivered today and, from what she'd learned first thing upon arriving at the house this morning, a three-piece orchestra.

It was a perfectly good waste of money in Evelyn's eyes. She figured the rug and curtains alone would probably pay her rent out in the poor part of the city for at least eight months.

And where was the birthday girl on the morning of this gluttonous coming-out party? Well, precious little Penny Pickett was asleep in her room. Here it was almost nine o' clock in the morning and Penny hadn't bothered to come out of her room yet. This was nothing new, though, as Penny often slept until ten or eleven in the morning. And why not? It wasn't like she had much of anything to do on any given day.

Evelyn was dusting the bottom of the stair rail, peering up to the second floor hallway, when Millie came walking by. She was dressed to the nines and talking with another well-dressed white lady with a pointy chin. When Millie passed by Evelyn, she stopped, turned to her maid, and sighed.

"Is the ever-loving girl still sleeping?" Millie asked.

"Yes ma'am, I guess so. I haven't seen a speck of her all morning."

"My sweet Lord," Millie said. The prissy woman next to her made a *hmmph* sound.

"Be a dear and go wake her, would you Evelyn?" Millie said.

"Yes ma'am." She tucked her duster into the tied drawstrings of her apron and started upstairs.

Evelyn honestly held no grudge toward Penny—nor George or Millie for that matter. The only thing that chapped her was that the parents spent money like people that had never lived without it and they were raising their daughter to be exactly the same. She supposed it came from a place of envy and she had to remind herself on a daily basis what the Good Book said about envy.

Evelyn came to the top of the stairs and walked down the finely carpeted hallway. She passed by the elegant vase sitting on a small table—both the vase and the table worth more than Evelyn could imagine, that did nothing but sit there to show proof of extravagances of the Picketts—on her way to Penny's room. She hesitated as she came to Penny's door. She wondered if she'd get the sweet version of Penny or the grumpy one. She figured it would be a sweet side of Penny today, being that this ridiculous party was about to be thrown in her honor.

She knocked on the door, waited a moment, and then said, "Penny! You best get out of bed before your mother comes and tosses you right out!"

There was no answer of any kind, not even the gentle slamming of a thrown pillow against the door—another tactic Penny had used in the past. Evelyn waited a beat and then leaned her head right against the door.

"Girl, you know they're throwing this big old party for you. If you're not downstairs soon, your parent's will take a mind to beat us both." She knocked again, louder this time, and added: "Now come on and get up!"

Evelyn nearly started walking away with that said. She'd taken a single step before she realized that something didn't feel quite right about this. Penny had always responded to Evelyn's attempts to wake her up, be it in a gentle and kind manner or a wretched and mean one. She started to wonder if the girl was sick, maybe with that summer flu some people had been catching a few weeks ago. And wouldn't that be one hell of a joke—the precious sixteen-year-old young lady sick on the day she's supposed to make some grand appearance to the public.

Curious, Evelyn stepped back to Penny's door. She knocked again and this time said nothing. She waited ten full seconds before she reached for the knob. "Penny…I don't know what you're up to in there, but I've knocked, okay? I've knocked and you're not answering, so I'm coming in."

Evelyn turned the ornate crystal doorknob and opened the door onto Penny's room. It was tidy like always, and morning sunlight came in through the room's only window on the right side. Penny was still in bed, mostly covered by the sheets. Evelyn opened her mouth to say something else but the feeling of something just not being right kept any words from coming out. Instead, she stepped closer to the bed. She saw that Penny was sleeping on her back, her head perfectly centered on the pillow. It was almost as if she was acting, making sure everything looked perfect and—

A gasp rose up in Evelyn's throat.

Penny's eyes were staring up at the ceiling, open wide and not blinking. Her head was so perfectly centered on the pillow and she was flat on her back because she had clearly not moved in quite some time.

"Penny…?"

But of course, Penny did not answer.

In fact, it was clear she would never speak again.

Evelyn ran out of the room and was screaming for George and Millie, even as they both continued to set up for a dead girl's party downstairs.

"You just try it, pal, and I'll make sure you're behind bars for a long time."

Ava Gold stared her son down as he was about to slip the remainder of his breakfast grits into the trash can. He looked guiltily at her but there was the merest trace of a smile on his face. He liked to hear his mom talk like a cop. He was still getting used to the fact that she was a detective now. So was Ava, actually.

"It's just one bite, Mom!" Jeffrey argued. "And they're so gross."

"You said it yourself. Just one bite. We don't waste food in this house, Jeffrey."

He was still grinning from the *behind bars* comment and gave in rather easily. He ate his last bite of grits and then went to the sink to wash the plate off.

"Good job," Ava said. "Now run brush your teeth. If we don't get out of here in the next five minutes, you're going to be late for school."

Jeffrey let out a sigh, but it didn't bother Ava. She knew he liked the rushing around. He liked it because the rushing meant that his mother now also had somewhere to be. Now that she was a detective, she had to work by a more rigid schedule. Rushing to get out of the door on time in the morning was a reminder of that and he usually had no issue with helping out.

Ava finished readying herself as she listened to Jeffrey quickly brushing his teeth. She'd been a detective for two weeks now and was slowly beginning to gain some respect within the precinct. But that wasn't exactly true of people on the street. Still, she always made sure to appear to be strong and confident for him, especially on the way to school. She knew that the newspapers and the talking heads on the radio were making a big deal about her sudden rise to the position of detective, as well as the entire New York Police Department's Women's Bureau. And that meant some of Jeffrey's school mates were surely giving him a hard time about his mother. She just hoped that the memories of his father and the stories Jeffrey had once told about him were enough to keep his friends from ribbing him too hard.

Ava looked herself over in the mirror and nodded to herself. She still wasn't the biggest fan of the uniform she had to wear. It was essentially a house dress, only somehow more uncomfortable than anything she'd willingly wear around her house. Still, it did make her look professional and for now, that was the most important thing.

She left the room and met Jeffrey in the hallway, carrying a stack of school books. "Are you going to be home in time to cook tonight or is Grandpa cooking?"

"I don't see why I'd be late," she said.

"Good. Grandpa isn't a very good cook. He thinks his cornbread is so good, but he burns the bottom and it tastes like coal."

"That's not very nice," Ava said.

"I know. Sorry. I'm glad he's living with us, though."

"Me, too," Ava said as she opened the front door. "And I'm glad he's letting you hang around the gym after school. But he's not letting you around any of those rougher men with foul mouths is he?"

"No. He's really careful about that and—"

Jeffrey was still talking, but Ava barely heard him. Her attention had been grabbed by the sheet of paper that had been placed on her front door. It was held in place by a tailor's tack. She plucked it free and unfolded it, already feeling that nothing good would come of it.

The note read: *A note to show that we know where you live. Tony 2 sends his regards.*

It was a note from the mob. In her sudden rise to the position of detective, she'd nearly overlooked the fact that she'd arrested and interrogated a member of the mob—a man that ended up having nothing to do with the murders she'd been investigating. And in terms of enemies, the mob was naturally among the worst to have.

She pocketed the note and tried her best to put on a smile for Jeffrey. He saw right through it, though. Ava sometimes forgot that her son had inherited his father's ability to properly read people's moods.

"What's wrong?" he asked. "What was the paper on the door?"

"Just a note for me," she said, placing a hand on his shoulder and escorting him along. "Work stuff."

And though she felt she played it off rather well, she could not help but draw Jeffrey a little closer to her side as they stepped out into the morning streets.

***

When she sat down behind her chair at work, she took the note out and placed it into the top drawer of her desk. There, it rested right on top of the letter someone within the precinct had left for her almost immediately after she was promoted to detective. It, like the letter from the mob, was nothing more than a thinly veiled threat—just some uncomfortable male trying to do what he could to feel like his was still the superior sex. She'd wasted far too much time trying to figure out who it might be from and, for some reason, the thought of it still worried her more than the new note from the mob.

The Women's Bureau office was starting to come alive as the morning passed by. Ever since she'd been promoted to detective, there was a strange and rather pleasant buzz in the air in the downstairs office. Ava had first worried that her sudden higher rank would cause bitterness with the other women, but so far she had received nothing but encouragement and support. It was a shame that the same wasn't true of the male officers. While no one was openly griping, she was still receiving a lot of hostility.

If her relationship with anyone in the WB had been altered in any significant way, it was the one she'd been forming with Frances. Officer Frances Knight had originally been tasked with showing Ava the ropes—a supervisor without actually being called such. But now that Frances no longer held that small position over Ava, things felt a little strained and off kilter.

Closing the drawer and keeping the mob's letter out of sight for now, Ava looked over in Frances's direction. She had her head down, reading a ream of paper that sat centered on her desk. As she watched Frances, Lottie came in through the door. She was looking stunning, as usual, despite the dress restrictions placed on all WB officers.

"G'morning ladies," Lottie said. "Already hard at work, I see."

Lottie sat down at her desk, two over from Ava. As she took her seat and looked to the few notes that had been placed on her desk, she sighed. When she looked to Ava, she seemed to wipe away any disappointment with a smile that seemed genuine enough.

"It's so good to know you're still trapped down here with us despite your rise to fame and superiority," she said.

"I think I prefer it down here," Ava said, meaning it. "It's much quieter, and a lot less...well, *male.*"

Lottie snickered at this and then whispered, "Though, there are a few up there I wouldn't mind bringing down here, that's for sure..."

Ava laughed, though she wasn't sure she agreed. She was starting to see most of the male officers as copies of one another—something she was not proud of but it came with the amount of evil looks and hostility she was getting from upstairs.

Across the room, the office phone rang on Frances's desk. She picked it up, still looking at the papers on her desk. "Women's Bureau, this is Officer Knight." She listened to the other end and within a few seconds looked up and met Ava's gaze. "Sure," Frances said, "Yes, of course." She then placed the receiver back on the cradle and said, "Gold you're needed upstairs in Minard's office. He says it's urgent."

She looked back to her papers, as if she honestly didn't care about the call at all. Still, the use of the word *urgent* had Ava getting to her feet and heading for the door.

"Well, it was good seeing you," Lottie said, giving a little wave. "I fear your time down in the basement with us may be a bit less permanent than it might seem."

Ava wasn't sure how to respond to this, so she kept quiet. As she made her exit from the WB offices, her nerves kicked up a bit. *Urgent,* she thought. *The last time Minard had asked for me with any sort of urgency was when I was thrown into the middle of the hatchet killer case...*

Her mind swirling with possibilities, Ava headed upstairs where within even just a few seconds, it all seemed like a totally different world.

CHAPTER TWO

She was both elated and a bit nervous to see that Frank Wimbly was already in Captain Minard's office when she arrived. She'd been unofficially partnered with him following their first case together and it seemed that they'd be getting something new right away, just a handful of days after managing to capture the hatchet killer. Frank's presence in the same office she'd been called into hinted at something pretty big on the horizon.

Frank greeted her with a quick smile as she took the remaining chair on the guest-side of Minard's desk. Thankfully, Minard did not seem to be in one of his hurried and angry moods today. Of course, it was still pretty early in the day.

"I've got a case I need both of you on," he said. "It's murder up on Fifth Avenue, concerning a very wealthy family. It has the potential to be pretty big and if the media gets ahold of it, it'll be a circus. Now, you two handled the hatchet murders with at least *some* degree of professionalism and somehow, the precinct came out smelling like roses. I'd like to see that same result at the end of this one."

The idea of dealing with the ultra-wealthy did not sit well with Ava but she would never actually speak up and say such a thing to Minard. Besides, she realized that she was being put on a large case and didn't want to do anything to jeopardize that. She couldn't help but wonder if she was being placed on it for the same reason she was finally given a break a little less than two weeks ago—for a bit of good PR for the force. She was now essentially the face of the NYPD's Women's Division. Were they just marching her out so the police force could remind the public of their bold moves?

Really, though, did it matter? She knew that if they *could* wrap this up successfully, it could mean huge things for her career and might even help to finally earn her some respect among her fellow officers.

"Who's the family?" Frank asked.

"The father is George Pickett. His sixteen-year-old daughter was found dead in her bed this morning. No clear signs of how it was done but it's looking like possible strangulation. Now make no mistake about this…Pickett is going to be all over your asses, watching everything you do. You're likely going to get yelled at and ridiculed and this is one situation where you're just going to have to smile, nod, and take it. Wimbly, you know this sort of case. You know money talks in this city and if it comes down to laws or money, money is going to win out every time."

"Yeah, that *is* an unfortunate truth about this city," Frank agreed.

Minard handed Frank a sheet of paper and seemed glad to be rid of it once it was in Frank's hand. Frank was wearing a derby hat that she'd seen him wear from time to time. She'd never asked or mentioned it, but she assumed he'd started wearing it more often because of the slight bit of hair loss that was starting to appear at the crown of his head.

"You know where it is?" Minard asked.

"Oh yeah, I know it."

"Then get moving. I have a feeling George Pickett is already going to be fuming that it's taken this long to get anyone over there…and we just got the call ten minutes ago." He then eyed Ava with what she thought looked like a strange sort of muted hope. "You got much experience on that side of town?"

"No, sir. Not much."

"Then please let Wimbly take the lead on this one. Got it? I'm putting you on this because the victim is female. Nothing more. I figured I should just be honest with that up front before your head gets too big."

"Yes, sir." It sounded like an insult at first but there was no fire in his voice. Maybe he was simply trying to make sure she knew her place—that she'd been given the keys to the kingdom and he felt it necessary to remind her.

Minard did not excuse or dismiss them, nor did he say goodbye. He simply looked down to his desk to the large pile of forms and papers. Frank caught Ava's gaze and nodded toward the door. He held it open for her and though it felt very anticlimactic, Ava realized that she was about to step out to start her second monumental case.

CHAPTER THREE

The Pickett residence was one of the remaining standouts from the cluster of Fifth Avenue mansions that had taken prominence in the 1890s. Granted, it wasn't much of a mansion anymore, but it was certainly one of the larger homes on the block. She supposed it would currently be considered a manor by most in the area. When Ava and Frank were greeted by the maid and stepped inside, Ava felt like she had just stepped into a very nice hotel rather than someone's home.

They entered through what she assumed was a foyer but felt more like a lobby. The hardwood floors had been recently cleaned and polished. She could smell a cleaning agent still clinging to the air. Ava started to truly take the place in, but she was unable to do so because she was distracted by the sheer number of people currently in the house. In the foyer alone, Ava counted six people. She could hear several other voices—including a very loud weeping one—coming from upstairs somewhere.

"Excuse me," Ava said to the maid. "But why are all of these people here?"

The maid shook her head and looked to the floor. She was an African American woman of about forty or fifty years of age. She had a very kind-looking face but she currently looked drained.

"Doesn't make a whole lot of sense, does it?" the maid said. "But her father won't send anyone away. Today was Penny's sixteenth birthday. Her parents had been planning her coming-out party for weeks now. Some of the folks here had arrived to help set up for the party and they just won't leave." She sneered in the direction of a few men standing in the corner, speaking quietly among themselves. "I guess they're afraid they won't have enough details to start talking about it over brandy and poker games tonight."

Ava understood and agreed with the comment. She decided right then and there that she liked this maid quite a bit. "What's your name?" she asked.

"Evelyn. Evelyn Johnson.

"Where is Penny's body, Evelyn?" Frank asked.

The maid took a single step back at the stern sound of Frank's voice. She looked almost pleadingly back to Ava, as if she wished the woman of the pairing was doing all of the talking. Still, she did her best to give them some answers.

"Some folks took her out a bit ago. The coroner. Maybe ten or fifteen minutes. I got the sense that Mr. Pickett wanted her out of here quickly. The mother—Millie—she took it hard. Damn near fainted when she saw Penny like that."

"Who discovered the body?" Frank asked.

"That was me, sir."

"Was there any blood?" Ava asked, trying to get back in control of the line of questioning. She wondered if Frank had even picked up on the fact that Evelyn was much more comfortable speaking with her. "Any sign that there might have been a fight?"

"No, nothing like that," Evelyn said. "The folks that took her out of here were talking about how she looked to have been strangled."

Frank thought about this for a moment before he gave Evelyn a little nod of appreciation. "Thank you. I assume the room is somewhere upstairs?"

"It is. Take the stairway in the parlor, though, not the one in the hallway."

"And the parlor is where?"

Evelyn sighed again, indicating she agreed; yes, this damn house was far too big. "To the left."

Frank and Ava left Evelyn to cater to the people in the massive foyer. As they made their way into the parlor, Ava saw large bookshelves stacked from end to end, as well as decorative vases and gorgeous pieces of artwork. Ava had always been able to appreciate the finer things; Clarence had once told her that he thought her love of music—jazz in particular—had something to do with it. But this house was different. Everything about the Pickett home spoke of extravagance—a family that spent excessive money simply because they could. As they made their way further inside, her mind was nearly assaulted by a vivid memory from her past. She could see herself at eight years of age, walking hand-in-hand with her mother down a street not too dissimilar from Fifth Avenue. They'd passed by a large house (not quite a mansion, though eight-year-old Ava would have not known the difference).

"Is that a castle, momma?"

"Not quite," her mother had answered.

"Do kings and queens live in there?"

She could still remember that look of contempt in her mother's face. *"No, Ava...but the men that own these types of places think they're kings anyway."*

Her mother's voice echoed in her head as she and Frank made their way out of the parlor and toward the stairway. There, Ava saw three more people. One was a woman sitting on the floor, her dress crumpled beneath her. She was heaving for air and her face was very red. Ava assumed this was the mother—Millie, according to the maid.

One of the other people was also very red in the face but not out of sorrow. No, this man looked absolutely livid. When he spotted Ava and Frank coming up the stairway, he stormed over to them at once. He had a well-trimmed moustache that almost looked as if it boxed his mouth off from the rest of his face.

"And who the bleeding hell are *you?*" this man asked.

Frank answered as nicely as he could though his suddenly-rigid posture was evidence that he did not like being spoken to in such a way. "I'm Detective Frank Wimbly," he said. "And this is my partner, Ava Gold."

"Partner?" the man asked, aghast. "A woman detective?"

"Yes. Is that going to be an issue?"

The man looked at a loss for words as the other two people behind him looked on. One was another man that looked just as privileged and refined as the man in front of Ava and Frank. The other was a waifish woman with a blank look on her face.

"Are you the father, sir?" Frank asked the mustached man.

"Yes. I'm George Pickett. And I have no idea why it took you so long to get here!"

Choosing to ignore this little jab, Frank came to the stairs with Ava following closely behind him. "Where's your daughter's bedroom, Mr. Pickett?"

"Upstairs," he snapped, pointing to the staircase. He looked appalled that a so-called woman detective would even be addressing him at all. "First room on the right."

Ava and Frank started up the stairs, and after a few steps, Ava turned back to the Picketts. "It's really none of my business," she said, "but this would all go a lot smoother if you didn't have all of these people here."

"You're absolutely right," George Pickett said. His face was redder than ever, his eyes pure orbs of fury. "It *is* none of your business. Now get upstairs and do your damned job."

"Come on, Gold," Frank whispered. He seemed to be doing everything he could to not face George Pickett, keeping his head low and his eyes straight ahead.

It took more restraint than it should have, but Ava managed to not say another word. She walked up the stairs to the dead girl's room, feeling both unwanted yet necessary at the same time.

CHAPTER FOUR

The room was tidy and smelled faintly of a flowery perfume. Other than the sheets being pulled back to remove the body, there wasn't much of a disturbance to the place. There were no signs of a struggle and everything looked to be in its proper place. Ava approached the bed and looked for any miniscule splatters of blood—anything to indicate someone had been attacked here—but there was nothing.

She noted Frank walking to the window, looking out onto high rises and expensive homes. He placed his face close to the glass, eyeing the frame and the bronze-colored lock closely.

"Doesn't look like anyone broke in," Frank said. "Not through the window, anyway."

Ava studied the bedroom door. She tested the knob and found that it turned freely. The lock itself, fashioned with a keyhole and just two bolts to hold it into the door, looked undisturbed. The hinges were also in solid condition. "The door doesn't look to have been forced either, assuming she may have locked it."

Frank looked to the bed, his arms crossed over his chest. Ava, meanwhile, looked the rest of the room over. The bureau against the left wall looked very old, the mirror scuffed and hazy but in a way that added to its allure. The little table by the edge of the window was just as tidy, the pen and pad sitting on it perfectly, as if deigned to sit there and never be used.

I'm curious," Ava said. "I never headed Clarence talk about break-ins or robberies in neighborhoods like this. Does it not happen often?"

"It happens from time to time, but it's rare. Even crooks are smart enough to know that if you get caught breaking in around here, the courts are going to treat you like shit. The owners of these sorts of places tend to have friends in high places—banks, courts, things like that." He gave her a brief smile and added, "Why do you ask?"

"There's no forced entry into the bedroom. It makes me think whoever killed her must have already been in the house. And with that party being planned, and so many people coming in and out, it doesn't seem too unlikely. I think we might need to talk to the maid again."

Frank nodded, already heading for the door. "I'll get her. George Pickett's reaction to a female detective doesn't make me think he's going to be much help if you go asking."

Frank stepped out and Ava continued to look around the room. She got down on her hands and knees, looking under the bed for any clues that might be there. But there was nothing. Not even strands of loose hair or dust, proof that the maid was very good at her job. Yet just as she was about to get back to her feet, she caught sight of something on the other side of the bed, against the wall. Viewing it from the lowered position while looking under the bed, it seemed rather obvious. But when she regained her feet and looked to the floor from a standing vantage point, what she had seen wasn't clear at all.

She walked over near the window and again got on her hands and knees, almost lying down on the floor. Sure enough, she was able to see it again. It was some sort of grease, just a smear of it no larger than one of her fingers, on the floor. It was a very light brown in color had gone unseen while standing on her feet because of the way the morning sunlight spilled across the hardwood floors. The sun made it almost transparent.

Ava touched her finger to the edge of the smear of grease and then placed it to her nose. It was mostly odorless, with the faintest traces of an odd, earthy smell. She supposed it could have been something overlooked by the maid and if that were the case, there was no telling how long it had been there. Of course, given the nature of what had recently happened on this room, Ava wasn't going to rule anything out.

As she again got back to her feet, Frank came back into the room. The maid, Evelyn, came in behind him. She looked a little shaken to be returning to the room, looking around as if she thought this might all have been some elaborate joke and they were finally going to let her in on the punchline.

"Thanks for coming up," Frank said, turning to Evelyn. "As I'm sure you can appreciate, we wanted to speak with you without the possibility of interference or objection from the family."

"Of course."

"When was the last time you saw the girl?" Frank asked.

"Penny was on the stairs, sketching something. She always liked to draw, though she wasn't very good at it."

"Do you know what time this might have been?"

"Shortly after nine last night," she said. "It was right before I left for the day."

"Is that when you usually leave?" Ava asked.

"Yes ma'am. I'm usually here between six in the morning and nine at night."

"Were both Mr. and Mrs. Pickett here when you left?"

"Yes."

"Did Penny have any siblings?" Ava asked.

"An older brother, name of Kelvin. But he's been out on his own for about a year or so now. Way I hear it, he should be on his way over here right now."

"And what about the people downstairs with the Picketts?" Frank asked. "Who are they?"

"Well, the people that are hugging on them and trying to help them make sense of it are the Duvalls. Mack and Betty. They have two sons floating around here somewhere."

"And what about the others that have come in and out for the party this morning?" Ava asked. "Do you have any idea about how many there have been?"

Evelyn took a moment to think it over. Ava appreciated the fact that the woman seemed to be doing her best to get every single detail right. "I'd say no more than eight. Decorators, a baker wanting to get details on a cake, a seamstress to check to see if Penny's dress needed to be taken in."

"Have you spoken with Mrs. Pickett at all since you found the body?" Ava asked. "Do you know when *they* last saw Penny alive?"

"Mrs. Pickett says she knows she was still awake and alive at nearly midnight because she could hear her pacing around a bit. She said Penny was quite nervous about this party."

"Has there been any sort of written record concerning the people that have been coming in and out of the house?" Frank asked.

"No, sir. But they started coming in around seven. I'd already been here for a bit. But I think I can get the names of everyone, if that's what you need."

"I think it might just come to that," Frank said. "Thank you so much for your help. You're free to get back to the family."

Evelyn made her exit, giving a polite little nod. Frank looked to Ava and said, "What do you think?"

"I think the killer might very well be in this house right now" Ava said. "And I have an even worse suspicion that it might have been a family member." She hesitated for a moment and then said, "Oh, and then there's this."

She stepped aside and pointed to the smear of odd grease on the floor. Frank squatted on his haunches and looked at the smear, doing the exact same thing Ava had done—touching it and then smelling it.

"Any idea what it is?" Frank asked.

"No. I was hoping you'd know."

"I don't think it's any sort of mechanic's grease. It's not some weird sort of makeup I don't know about, is it?"

"No," she said, unable to suppress her small smile.

"You see it anywhere else?"

She shook her head, and they started scanning the room for more of it. When it was clear they weren't going to find more, Frank shrugged. "Could be hundreds of different things. But I think the fact there's hardly any means that it may not be important."

Ava thought this was the case, but hated to simply ignore it outright. With no clues, it felt irresponsible to rule the smear of grease out completely. She stored it in the back of her mind and then looked to the doorway.

"Time to start asking questions?"

"Yeah, I believe it is," Frank said. "And I won't even lie to you; men like George Pickett are not going to take kindly to it, especially with a woman detective involved."

"I think I'll be okay. I'm pretty tough."

He grinned at her said, "Oh, I know. Just…remember I warned you."

They headed downstairs and Ava was glad that George Pickett was nowhere to be found. Instead, there was Millie, still weeping. Frank gave Ava a gentle nudge in Millie's direction. Apparently, he'd caught on to the apparent truth that women tended to respond better when she was asking the questions.

"Mrs. Pickett, where would be the best place to conduct interviews with everyone currently in the house?"

She shrugged but finally managed to say, "George's study I suppose." She pointed a shaking finger down the hallway. "George is already in there."

Frank started in that direction right away. And though Ava hated to leave poor Millie Pickett to her sorrow, she knew a pesky detective in her ear was likely the last thing she needed. She followed Frank down the hallway and came to the first open door along the hallway. Ava was almost irritated with how beautiful the room was.

George Pickett's study was gorgeous and spacious, but it was also a fitting illustration of his tendency towards extravagance and pretentiousness. His desk was the size of one of the smaller boats that came in and out of the harbor. It was made of a dark wood that Ava could not identify and looked as if it were polished every single day. A thick ledger sat on it, as well as an ornate lamp. There were bookshelves on each wall, many of the spines glossy and new, showing that they had never been opened and had likely been purchased for nothing more than decoration.

George Pickett, though, seemed like a perfect fit for the room. He stood behind the desk, ignoring the chair completely, and lorded over the room like a king. His grief and anger seemed to project throughout the room as Ava and Frank also opted to stand rather than sit down in the five other chairs placed around the room.

"Let me make sure I am understanding you *perfectly clear,*" George said. He was trembling with fury. "You are accusing me and my wife of killing our daughter?"

"No, not at all," Frank said. "I've not accused anyone at this point. But given that your wife states that Penny was moving around and very much alive just shy of midnight, we have to go by what we know. And that is that in the eight hours that passed between midnight and nine this morning, someone murdered her by strangling her. There are no signs of forced entry in her room or at the front door. That leads me to believe that the killer was someone within the house. And being that so many people have come in and out in the last few hours, I think it is *very* important that anyone in the house right now is not allowed to leave."

"I'm no fool," George said. "Yes, I can see that clearly. But what that does is place my wife and myself in the pool of suspects."

"Technically, yes," Ava said. "But an alibi would clearly free you of suspicion."

"Well, the only alibi I have is that I was in bed shortly after eleven last night. I then woke up just after six and started tending to this party."

"And was your wife in bed with you the entire time?"

"Likely not. She gets up to relieve herself about two times a night. I assume that's when she says she heard Penny moving just shy of midnight. And if you—"

He faltered here and the fury on his face morphed into sorrow. His arms went rigid as his palms rested on the desk. It looked to Ava like he was struggling to hold himself up—as if being questioned in such a way had brought the full realization of the morning on him. He looked to both of them as if he'd just been physically attacked and then left the desk to make his way across the room. Before he reached the door, he'd started weeping. He covered his face, as if the act of crying might make him weaker in the eyes of anyone that might see. The sounds of his crying faded as he hurried away down the hall elsewhere into the house.

"As far as alibis go, it's not a very strong one," Frank said.

"Not even if the wife can back it up," Ava added. "Even if she's a light sleeper and woke up if George got out of bed, would she tell us if she thought it might make him look bad?"

"Doubtful."

Ava was about to suggest they go speak to the Duvalls, who had not objected when they'd been asked to stay. But before she could get the thought out of her mouth, two people came in through the office door. The first was Millie Pickett. Though she looked much better than she had when Ava and Frank arrived half an hour ago, she was still shaky and weak. She was being escorted into the room by a young man that bore a striking resemblance to George. This, Ava assumed, was the older son Evelyn had mentioned.

Millie fell into the first chair she came to, and the young man stayed by her side, holding her hand.

"You're the son, I take it?" Frank said.

"I am. Kelvin Pickett. And look…I know you have a job to do, but you can't just accuse my parents like this."

"As I've been saying over and over this morning," Frank said, "I'm not accusing anyone. We're just trying to get the story straight. Kelvin, where do you live?"

"A little town about an hour away from here. Wyatt River."

"And you've just arrived here?"

"Yes. I've been here for about three minutes. Long enough to see and hear my father break in half over this."

Ava could see that Kelvin had some of his father's stubborn defiance in him and thought she might be able to use it to their advantage. All she had to do was swing it so that Kelvin truly didn't think he or his parents were being directly targeted. She stepped a bit closer to the chair where Millie sat and lowered her voice.

"Kelvin, how well do you know the Duvalls?"

Kelvin looked confused for a moment but then Ava saw the shift she'd been expecting. He looked to his mother for just a moment before looking back to Ava. "I know Mack pretty well, I guess. I don't know his wife at all, really. Mack and my father are competitors in the business world, but they've always been really good friends. They would—"

Millie Pickett took her son's hand and patted it affectionately. "You don't need to answer their questions," Millie said. "I hate that you're even caught up in this. You need to be…you need to be grieving…"

At this, she also broke into a fresh bought of weeping. Being brand new to this sort of scene, Ava had never been forced to speak to someone so soon after losing a loved one. It made her think of how she felt when she'd learned of Clarence's death. It had taken her several days to fully accept that he was gone, that he was simply no longer a part of her life—of this world. It made her feel a little wretched to be questioning this family less than three hours after losing their daughter and sister.

"I'm taking her out of here," Kelvin said. He sneered at them but Ava thought she saw something very close to respect in his eyes, She wondered if he might be the only one in the family that realized they were asking these questions because they were trying to find the person who killed his sister.

"Kelvin," Frank said, "would you please send in the Duvalls?"

"Yes," he said quickly. Ava could see the emotion riding under his calm façade and wondered how much longer it would be before it broke. He hurried his mother out of the room, her head sinking into the crook of his shoulder.

"If Kelvin has a home in Wyatt River," Ava said, "I'd say he has a pretty solid alibi."

"Better than *I was asleep all night,* that's for sure," Frank added. "I do find it sort of interesting that Mack Duvall and George Pickett are direct competitors yet also on a very friendly basis."

"Friendly sure," Ava said. "But friendly enough to hang out at the house even after your friend's daughter has been murdered?"

"Yeah, it seems a little strange, doesn't it?"

Before either of them could comment on this further, the Duvalls arrived and stormed through the doorway. Mack Duvall had the same *I-dare-you* look on his face that Ava had seen on George Pickett. She took a deep breath and prepared herself, keeping in mind that with this rich crowd before her, any cross word out of her mouth might very well cost her the detective position she'd miraculously earned.

CHAPTER FIVE

Frank didn't like the look of Mack Duvall. He was just the sort of man that looked arrogant at first glance—the sort you just knew was going to turn out to be a grade-A asshole. His wife walked sheepishly behind him, dressed in a delicate white gown that Frank supposed had been intended as her wardrobe for Penny Pickett's coming out party.

"I certainly hope you have some answers," Mack Duvall said. "Because if you intend to even suggest that we had anything to do with this, I'll have to contact your direct supervisor."

Oh, and I'm sure you would, too, Frank thought. Instead, though, he said, "Not at all. As you can imagine, the Picketts are distraught over Penny's death and we were hoping to get information out of you so we wouldn't have to burden them with it."

"Of course," Betty Duvall said.

Mack Duvall looked to her with a distrusting glance. Apparently, the Duvall home was the sort where a woman was to be seen, not heard. As Mack regarded the detectives, another figure came in through the door. Frank could tell it was a Duvall right away; the boy had the sharp nose and strawberry blonde hair of his mother.

"James, you don't need to be in here," Mack said. "Go on out and see what you can do for the Picketts."

"They sent me in here. They want to be alone, Father."

Frank wasn't sure why, but it seemed that Mack did not like this bit of news. He looked awkwardly between his son and his wife, fuming. Beside Frank, Ava started the line of questioning, and he was nervous for her. He had no idea how she might react if a wealthy man like Mack Duvall or George Pickett said something inappropriate or sexist to her.

"Mr. and Mrs. Duvall, can we assume you were simply here to support the family during their big day for Penny?"

"That's right," Mack snapped. "We got here shortly after eight o' clock to see if there was anything we could do to help."

"Kelvin Pickett told us your families are very good friends," Ava said.

"We are. George and I have been good friends ever since our college days."

"But you're competitors at work. Yes?" Frank asked.

"We're bankers at different establishments," Mack said, speaking as if he were explaining it to a five year-old. "Yes, there is always competition, but it is all in good fun."

"How often would you say your families get together just to spend time and enjoy each other's company?" Ava asked.

The look on his face made it quite clear that Mack Duvall did not like the idea of a woman questioning him in such a way. He looked almost disgusted by it, but he still managed to answer.

"At least once a week. But oftentimes, Betty will come over to have tea with Millie on Wednesdays."

"You must be very close, then," Frank said. "And very good, close friends to stay by their side in such a sorrowful moment."

"Yes," Betty said. "I told Millie I would stay here to send away people that came for the party. Evelyn and I have just started telephoning the guests to let them know."

"You have two children, correct?" Ava said, looking to James as if asking with her eyes where their other son might be.

"Yes," Betty said. She opened her mouth to say something else, but Mack cut her off rather quickly.

"Another son," he said. "His name is Cole and he's ten years old. He's currently playing jacks in the courtyard and that's where he will stay."

Ava caught herself clenching her fists. She truly did not like this despicable man, but she knew she had to keep a calm façade or face unnecessary trouble.

"He'd only make fun of me anyway," James said, seeming both sad and embarrassed.

"Why's that?" Frank asked.

Apparently, James did not see the look of absolute scorn his father shot toward him. The boy was far too concerned with the detectives, perhaps a little enamored by the fact that he had somehow been caught up in the middle of a murder case. And even though his cheeks reddened as he seemed to understand he may have spoken out of turn, he answered with a slight tremble in his voice.

"Because I was supposed to marry her."

Frank and Ava looked at one another and for a moment, it was almost as if they were speaking with their minds. *Oh, okay,* they both seemed to say with their eyes. *Isn't it pretty damned funny that no one has bothered to mention that yet?*

The room went quiet for a while and Ava could all but feel a little wave of rage emanating from Mack Duvall toward his oldest son.

James picked up on it and his cheeks went event redder. He knew he'd messed up and was waiting for the eventual explosion. To Mack Duvall's credit, he did not explode. In fact, he slowly walked over to his son and whispered something in his ear. James nodded, went to the corner of the room, and sat down. He looked quite unhappy, making Ava assume Mack had whispered the boy's punishment into his ear.

"I'll ask the obvious question," Frank said, eyeing both of the Duvall parents. "Given that the bride-to-be was murdered while she slept, why did no one find it important to tell us that your son was going to marry her?"

"Because it was something that would be announced at a later date," Mack said, speaking to him as if he were lecturing a two-year-old. "There would be her coming-out party and maybe a few months after that, we'd announce their engagement."

"When was it decided they would get married?" Ava asked. The question was out of her mouth before she had time to think about it. The idea of an arranged marriage between two sixteen year olds in what was supposed to be a civilized America had her blood racing, momentarily breaking through her attempts at staying calm.

"That is a family matter and none of your concern at all," Mack said.

Ava knew she was going to have to step away or she was going to end up saying something she might regret. Worse, she may end up doing something with her clenched fists. She could see Frank looking at her out of the corner of his eye, as if he could tell she was struggling with the situation.

"We're only trying to get to the bottom of this murder," Frank said.

Before Mack Duvall could come back with some snide and rude comment, Ava excused herself. She started for the door and said, "I believe I'll go check on Mrs. Pickett."

Before she left, she caught the condescending look on Mack Duvall's face. He seemed pleased that the woman detective was doing what a woman *should* do. Stay out of the way. Stay quiet. His poor wife was still looking at the floor as if in search of something she'd dropped.

Ava had no intention of going to check on Millie Pickett, though. When she left George Pickett's office, she could hear Millie crying off somewhere to the right. Ava went back to the large foyer and then to the left, where a gorgeous set of double doors led out into the small courtyard. It was really just a glamorized backyard, complete with paver stones, well-maintained rose bushes, and a decorative concrete fountain. She stepped out into the space and, just as Mack Duvall had said, saw a small boy perched on his knees, playing jacks. As she approached him, he was in the process of bouncing the ball. The red ball bounced and he swept up three of the silver jacks with expert precision.

"Woah," Ava said, putting on her best impressed-adult act. "That was pretty fast."

The boy turned quickly around, a smile of pride on his face. Ava felt comfortable when she drew closer to him. Even when Clarence had been alive, she'd usually been the one to interact with Jeffrey on tough matters. And over the past few weeks, she thought she'd done a pretty good job of walking him through the loss of his father. She was good with children and tended to know how to talk to them based on the situation.

"You're James's brother, right?" Ava asked.

"Yeah."

"What's your name?"

He frowned a bit but then seemed to decide that Ava was safe to talk to. "Cole Duvall. What's yours?"

"I'm Ava Gold," she said.

"Are you here to help because Penny died?"

"That's right."

Cole nodded, now just rolling the red ball back and forth between his hands. "Everyone is really upset about it, huh?"

"Yes, it's very sad when we lose someone. Mr. and Mrs. Pickett are very sad right now. I think it means a lot to them that your parents are here to spend time with them." She waited a moment, trying to choose the right words before continuing. "But your parents spend a lot of time here, don't they?"

"Oh boy, yeah," Cole said. "Me and James, too."

"Do you like that? Do you like spending time with the Picketts?"

"Sometimes. Mrs. Pickett is awful nice, but sometimes Penny was mean. Not like teasing or nothing, just…sometimes she didn't want to be around people."

"Were there ever arguments about it?" Ava asked, not sure how many more questions she'd be able to ask before he got suspicious. She guessed him to be eight or nine years old, so it wasn't easy to guess his level of secrecy.

"Not until last night."

Ava felt that she'd gotten to something important without really even trying. She kept her suspicions under control as she went on, though. "What happened last night, Cole?"

"Penny was really mad at everyone." He was bouncing the ball again, speaking as if he were doing nothing more than explaining the rules of jacks. "Penny had told everyone that she liked James just fine but didn't want to marry him. She said she wanted to marry whoever she wanted, and when she was older."

"And both of your parents were here for that?"

Cole nodded enthusiastically. "Yes, and Mommy was crying. She was really sad. But it made Daddy really mad. He was shouting and that got Mr. Pickett to shouting and—"

He was interrupted by a booming voice from behind them. "Step away from my son right now, you meddlesome witch."

Ava did not have to turn around to know that it was Mack Duvall. She stood slowly to face him. He was once again red in the face and for a second or two, Ava thought he might come charging at her. And Lord help her, she almost *wanted* him to. She was already tiring of these rich pricks thinking they owned the world and that their word was the absolute law.

"One word of caution," Ava said. "Mind the way you speak to the police."

"I think you should mind the way you speak to your superiors. I told you I did not want my son involved in this and here you are, talking to him."

She stepped closer to him and it seemed to confuse him. "And now I know why," she said. "I got more useful information out of Cole than I did you, your wife, or either of the Picketts. You want to tell me about the argument that occurred here last night?"

"That is *none of your concern!*" he shouted. "If you and your partner don't leave at once, I'll—"

"You'll do absolutely nothing," Ava said. "First of all, it isn't your house. And maybe your money has blinded you to this, but despite your riches, you're not above the law. As a matter of fact, if I wanted to *make* you come to the station to answer some questions, I easily could."

He snarled at her and came forward, taking her bait. "How…dare…you…"

Ava acted quickly, swiping her cuffs from her belt and slapping one of them on Mack's right arm. By the time he realized what was happening, she gave him a quick spin around, pulled his other arm behind him and secured the other cuff.

"What do you think you're doing?" he bellowed. Suddenly, his anger turned to something else—something like bewilderment. It seemed that he legitimately could not believe he'd been bested.

"You're under arrest, Mr. Duvall."

"For what, in God's name?"

The commotion had drawn a crowd to the courtyard doors. Both of the Picketts were standing there, George looking as if he were watching a dragon roaming about his courtyard. Millie Duvall was also looking out and Ava thought she saw the faintest bit of a smile at the corners of her mouth for just a second.

Frank stood behind them and Ava ignored the look of horror on his face. As she ushered Mack Duvall forward and he continued to scream and protest, though, Frank's expression changed. And by the time they were halfway back down the Pickett's hall and to the front door, Frank was the one escorting Mack. The man continued to scream and wail about his innocence and how this was so unfair and unjust, but not even the people they passed in the street seemed to care.

"Even if you come out of this smelling like roses," Ava said, "everyone is going to remember this temper tantrum you're throwing. Take my advice and shut your mouth."

Mack looked at her as if he would very well kill her if given the chance. And though she supposed she understood the reaction given his status, it also made her think this man might very well indeed be capable of murder.

CHAPTER SIX

When Ava and Frank hauled Mack Duvall into the precinct, Ava was very much aware that she may have made a mistake by arresting the man. The wide eyes and whispered voices throughout the precinct only solidified this suspicion. But she had quickly learned to look past such things. As a female detective that earned her place in record time and by total luck of the draw and circumstance, she *knew* there was always going to be attention on her. The balance she was trying to strike was knowing when to ignore that attention and when to consider that it might be warranted.

As she opened the interrogation room door and Frank ushered Mack inside, Ava managed to look past such worries. She was finding that she enjoyed this part of the job—not because it gave her the right to question people--but because this was where she really felt the puzzle of it all starting to slip into place. This was where the pieces were found, where the mystery could truly start to be solved.

When Mack took the seat behind the scarred oak table in the center of the room, he did so with a heavy sort of thud—yet again bringing Ava's temper tantrum comparison to mind. It was clear he wasn't used to being in situations like this and he was trying to figure out which sort of approach to take—stubborn and mean or trying to play the victim. Currently, he was failing at both.

"We'll start simple enough," Ava said. "I want to know why no one bothered telling us that your son was supposed to be married to Penny Pickett."

He struggled with saying anything. She could tell he was working his way through his options, trying to figure out what was going to make him look best when this was all over. Frank apparently knew this as well because he crossed his arms and leaned against the wall trying to seem as casual as he could.

"Look," Frank said. "People already saw you cuffed. Maybe not many, but some. The easier you make the next several minutes, the bigger chance you come out of this looking helpful. It's up to you, really. The longer you're here being stubborn, the fishier it's going to seem to anyone that finds out you were hauled in."

"Really?" he said. "I don't recall having much of a choice when I was arrested by this crazy dame!"

"That's not quite how being arrested works," Ava said dryly. "Now, how about answering my question."

He took another ten seconds to glare at Ava, as if he were trying to burn a hole through her with his hatred. Finally, he said, "Because in these modern times, people frown on arranged marriages. Well, in this country, anyway. But that's sort of ignorant. Money marrying money just ensures that both families can continue their legacy. And in the case of myself and the Duvalls, no one was in it against their will. We both thought it was a good idea. George and I even planned a merger of our businesses around it. If it all worked out, our families could be set for generations."

"Based on what Cole told me, Penny wasn't a big fan," Ava said. "And being the bride-to-be, I'd think her voice would matter."

"She was too young. There's no way she could understand legacies and how to better her own future."

Just when Mack Duvall hit one low, he seemed to find a way to go even lower. Aside from the man that had killed her husband, she wasn't sure she'd ever detested a man more.

"And when was the wedding supposed to take place?" Frank asked. He'd stepped up to take the lead and Ava thanked him for it. She wasn't sure how much more she could speak with the goon.

"We'd planned it for the month after she turned eighteen. The plan was to have her and James be seen in public as a couple here and there between her coming-out party and her eighteenth birthday, with an engagement somewhere during her seventeenth year."

"Was Penny ever on board with this?" Frank asked.

"Lord yes. When we first presented her and James with the plan about a year ago, she was thrilled. She and her mother were talking about wedding dresses and wedding ceremonies, and honeymooning in Paris."

"But last night…?" Frank asked. Ava noticed how he left the comment open, not really asking a question, but leaving the question open-ended for Mack to answer. She liked the idea and stored it away for future use.

"Last night as we were all trying to plan the party for today, she had a change of heart. She said she only wanted to ever get married for love, not because two families thought it was a good idea."

"And I take it you and Mr. Pickett didn't take kindly to this, correct?"

Mack sighed and nodded. "I admit, I lost my head and said things I shouldn't have said. In fact, George and I talked about it this morning and it was all forgiven. We made plans to speak with both Penny and James a few days after the party."

"So you felt the need to have George forgive you?" Ava asked. "Does that mean he didn't exactly take your side?"

"Well, no. Not right away. Then again, George always was a pushover when it came to Penny. We were both blindsided by Penny's change of heart, and we took it differently He saw a daughter in distress before he saw plans for the future of his family in the many years to come. I understand it; but in that moment, I did not see it."

"Are you on good terms now?" Frank asked.

"As far as I know. We had the discussion about an hour and a half before Penny's body was found. Naturally, it has not come up, as he has worse things to worry about."

Frank looked over to Ava before he took a single step towards the table. "Mr. Duvall, the questions I'm about to ask you are not meant to sound accusatory. We'd have to ask the same questions of *anyone* in this room that was currently your position. So let that settle in before you get defensive."

Mack looked very uncomfortable, but gave a curt little nod. Ava was pretty certain the man knew what was coming and was squirming in his seat because of it.

"When did you leave the Pickett home last night?"

"I don't know an exact time, but it was shortly before eleven."

"Was the party the topic of conversation most of the night?"

"It was. Near the end we were simply enjoying some brandy and laughing, talking about nonsense. But other than that, yes—it was all about the party."

"And did you go straight home after you left there?"

"Yes, we did."

Ava enjoyed watching Frank at work. He spoke softly and casually but there was something about the way he stood over the table that seemed silently intimidating. She was beginning to understand that there was a lot she could learn from him.

"Did you go straight to bed when you arrived home?"

"Yes. I brushed my teeth and change into my bedclothes."

"You and your wife both?"

"Yes." Mack was starting to get antsy now, growing a bit more tense with each pointed question.

"Do you know what time your family arrived at the Pickett house this morning?"

"I arrived just before seven, but Millie and the boys arrived a bit earlier. I was a bit behind because I had to meet with a man at the bank."

"So early?"

"Yes, because I figured my day would be consumed by this party. It was a very important matter—a deal over some land."

"Who saw you come in?" Ava asked. "Did you knock or just let yourself in?"

"I let myself in. We are very close friends."

"Did anyone see you come in?" Frank asked.

"I'm not sure. But I do believe the maid saw me—Evelyn, I believe her name is."

Ava considered it all as Frank continued to question him about his whereabouts yesterday afternoon. If Evelyn had indeed seen him enter and there was at least one person that could account for where Mack had been at any given time, it would go a long way towards clearing him for this morning. But if he had just walked in this morning, what would have stopped him from doing so at any point last night when the Picketts had been asleep? Even with the doors locked, might the families be close enough for Mack to know how to get in?

As Frank brought things to a close, Ava asked one more question. She figured it would seem obvious enough, but would also go a long way toward telling what avenue to pursue next.

"Before last night's argument between you and Mr. Pickett, had you ever argued to that extent before?"

"Not at all." He was still looking at her with great anger, but there was something in that look that seemed to be softening. He was quite sure he was on the verge of being let go—and that might very well be the truth. "Maybe a disagreement here and there on how to best present business practices or how to treat employees, but even that was always nothing more than good-natured ribbing."

It was what she had expected. She nodded and smiled, making her way out of the room. She could feel his eyes at her back and she couldn't help but wonder if he knew what he'd just confessed—that last night's argument between he and Pickett might be a bit more relevant than he thought.

CHAPTER SEVEN

"You want to tell me what you're thinking?" Frank asked as they left the station and headed back for Fifth Avenue.

"The Duvalls and the Picketts never argue. Mack Duvall said that himself. But the one thing they *did* argue about was the fate of George Pickett's daughter. Even with the threat of whatever financially successful merger they had planned going to pot, George Pickett stood up for his daughter. It makes me think there might be some hidden resentment there. Maybe if we dig just enough…"

"Pickett will reveal anything worth revealing about Duvall," Frank finished for her.

"Possibly."

"That's some very good thinking, Gold."

"Thanks," she replied, looking to the street ahead of them. Her father's gym was two blocks ahead. It was a tiny bit out of their way, but she wanted to stop by. "I want to make a quick stop before we head back to the Pickett house," she said. "Is that okay with you?"

"Sure. We have time. It'll be another fifteen minutes or so before Duvall is done with all of the paperwork to get him out of the station. So long as we get back to the Picketts' before he does, I think we'll be okay."

"You don't think George will talk if Mack is there?"

"No, I don't. Because while he is mourning his daughter, he's also likely thinking about his own image in all of this as well."

"What the hell is wrong with wealthy people?" Ava asked.

"No clue. I've never had the misfortune of being one." Frank smiled at his own joke as they crossed the street and neared Roosevelt's Gym.

Being near eleven in the morning, the place was quite dead. A single man stood in the back working on the punching bags and a young man worked quickly at a jump rope near the rings. As for her father, he was sitting on a small stool by the corner of that same ring, thumbing through the day's newspaper. As the door closed behind her, she noted that Frank had elected to stay outside and wait. She wasn't sure if this was his way of giving her privacy or if he didn't want to go through the awkwardness of the situation.

When Roosevelt saw her, he got up and placed the paper on the stool. "This is a big surprise," he said. "What brings you to this part of town? Not here to arrest these gym bums, are you?"

"No, not today, Dad. But there's something I need to tell you…a favor, I suppose. And I need you to do your best not to worry too much about it."

"Okay…" Roosevelt said, clearly skeptical.

"There was a note on my door when I left for work this morning. It was a threatening note from the mob…though I don't even really know if it was real. It could have been someone just playing a mean trick." But even as she said this, she doubted it was actually true. She'd known it was the real thing the moment she saw it.

Apparently, her father felt the same without even seeing it. "I don't think anyone would be brave enough to prank a detective in such a way *or* pretend to be the mob. Besides, who else would be able to find where you live?"

"Dad, I'm just telling you so—"

"Damn, Ava…this could be serious. I mean, think of Jeffrey."

"I am. And that's why I'm here. I was hoping you could get Jeffrey from school today. let him hang out here like usual. And then, if it's not too much trouble, let him stay with you, in your apartment, until I get home. Just keep him safe…just in case."

"Of course, I will. But Ava…if you think this mob thing is for real, you need to tell your superiors. You can't just live under it."

"I'll handle it, Dad." Though honestly, she had no idea what to do. She wasn't going to tell Frank because it would make him worry *and* create a fissure in what was becoming a promising career for her. The last thing she needed after the last case she'd been involved with was more drama attached to her name.

"Be careful out there, okay?"

"I always am."

She leaned forward and kissed his cheek, a gesture that took him by surprise. She then left, the sounds of the punching bag and the jump rope slapping the floor escorting her out. When she rejoined Frank, she started walking right away. He didn't miss a step, speeding up to make sure he was always just slightly ahead of her.

"Everything okay?" he asked.

"Yeah. Just wanted to check in on him."

Frank seemed satisfied with this answer. He said nothing else as he remained one step ahead of her, leading them back to Fifth Avenue.

* * *

Knowing what had occurred in the Pickett house and having already stepped inside made it seem like an entirely different place. Ava nearly felt like she was about to enter some haunted Gothic manor rather than a Fifth Avenue home. As she looked over the gorgeous façade—the expertly laid brick, the large windows, and long and elegant stairs leading to the front door—Ava had a thought.

"Hold on before going in," she told Frank. "I want to check on something."

She started to the side of the building, which was separated from the next home over by a large and well-maintained strip of grass roughly half an acre long. She then turned and went to the back of the house. She saw the brick wall that blocked off most of the courtyard but even closer to her was what she had been hoping to see all along.

The fire escape almost looked like a blemish, even on the backside of the house and out of everyone's sight. She walked over to it and reached up, though it was just a bit too tall for her to grab. Frank did it for her, saying nothing and not making a big show of it. When the ladder had clacked down, she slowly started climbing it. It wasn't very sturdy. She imagined anyone heavier than one hundred and seventy-five pounds might think twice about climbing it. When she reached the little iron walkway that ran beneath Penny's room as well as two others, she tried each and every window. She found them all locked and could see no obvious signs of forced entry. She'd pretty much expected this but was happy to have the option fully eliminated.

As she started back down the ladder, she heard a commotion from the street. There were several voices, one louder than the others—and the loud voice seemed to be distressed.

"You okay to get down by yourself?" Frank asked. "I want to check on this."

"Yeah, I'm good. Right behind you."

This was true enough. Ava managed to climb down the unsteady iron ladder with ease. She came up behind Frank just as he rounded the corner of the Picketts' house, looking out onto the street. To their left, about half a block away from the front door of the Pickett residence, three well-dressed men were standing shoulder to shoulder. One held a briefcase and another one held one of those pretentious canes, used by men that did not really need them at all. They were speaking in angry tones to a fourth man that was pressed against a lamppost, doing his best to stand his ground but quite scared.

The difference between the four men was rather stark. The man against the lamppost was dressed in disheveled clothes and had scraggly, long hair that was in need of a wash. He looked very out of place in this Fifth Avenue scene and it took Ava only a single second to understand what was happening here.

The man with the cane was holding it out almost like a sword, pointing it towards the man. "You go back to your side of town! Back to where you came from!"

"Nothing but a damned sewer rat," the third man said, to which the man with the briefcase laughed heartily. As if encouraged by his friend's laughter, the third man reached down into a nearby flowerbed, tore up a small patch of earth, and tossed it at the man. It struck his leg and the trio of wealthy men laughed.

The anger that flooded Ava took her by surprise. It took Frank by surprise, too; when Ava went rushing past him, his eyes went wide with surprise. "So it now takes three men to deal with one rat, does it?" Ava asked.

The men wheeled around at her and the looks on their faces made her even angrier. They were not embarrassed that they had been caught acting so immaturely. The man with the cane actually looked mad that he'd been interrupted from his fun.

"Look here, you nosy broad," the man with the cane said. "What business is it of…"

He stopped here, his eyes narrowing and then widening when he saw her holstered gun. He then saw Frank just behind her. At this, the man's jaws clenched tightly shut.

"I think you all owe this man an apology."

"He's clearly trespassing," the man who had thrown the dirt said. "He has no business here."

Frank took a few steps forward, backing Ava up, and said: "So what if he does not live around here? What crime is he committing?" The fact that Frank was quickly taking her side meant a great deal to her. For a moment, she wasn't sure how to react.

All three men looked to one another, as if hoping one of their friends might have an answer that would allow them to leave this situation without being the ones in the wrong.

"All three of you, move on about your business," Frank said. There was more bass in his voice than Ava was accustomed to hearing.

The men did as asked, the one with the briefcase crossing the street and heading in a different direction than his friends. Ava and Frank stood there for a moment, watching them leave. The man that had been accosted remained standing against the lamppost, looking wildly back and forth between the detectives and his three harassers.

"Thank you kindly," the man said. He looked very embarrassed but the gratitude in his eyes was genuine. It wasn't until he spoke that Ava realized he was likely an immigrant that had simply not learned the layout of the city. He had a European accent that, while not thick, stood out easily.

Hell of a welcome to America, Ava thought.

"Can we help you get somewhere?" Ava asked. "Are you lost?"

The man shook his head, hanging it slightly, and walked away quicky. Ava's heart broke for him and she had half a mind to go track down those three men that had been harassing him just to put a scare into them.

Apparently seeing this in her, Frank softly placed his hand on her arm. "Come on," he said. "Let's have a word with the Picketts before George Duvall shows up again."

Even with anger still thrumming in her, Ava knew this was the best thing to do. She turned back towards the Picketts' home and, with the thought of that poor immigrant in her head, hated everything about the place. But she did her best to look past that as she and Frank walked inside, still looking for answers as to why Penny Pickett was murdered.

CHAPTER EIGHT

The house felt different now. It was a place where grief had made its rounds and the rooms were now occupied by it—a thick silence that Ava felt pressing against them as they walked into the large den space. In the time they'd been gone, a local minister had come to visit. He was sitting with Millie, holding her hand, reading from the book of Psalms. Millie nodded here and there, wiping tears away from her face.

As they stood by and waited, a man approached from behind. Ava turned and saw Kelvin standing behind them, peering into the den. "I take it you're convinced it wasn't Mack?" he asked.

"We're convinced of nothing just yet," Ava said.

"If it helps, I don't think he did it. Mack may talk a very big game but he doesn't like to get his hands dirty. Even in business, when he has to have a hard conversation with someone, he sends someone else to do it. I have a hard time thinking he'd kill anyone, much less Penny."

He stuttered a bit at the sound of his sister's name and Ava could tell that he was using every ounce of his available strength not to cry. She assumed he was trying his very best to stay strong for his parents. Poor Millie Pickett looked like she was going to be out of sorts for a very long time.

"Where is your father?" Ava asked. "We'd really like to meet with him while there is no one else around to distract him."

"He's in his study right now. But let me warn you…Betty and James are sitting just outside of the office. I think they assumed you'd be back. They're quite upset about you arresting Mack."

"And what about you?" Frank asked. "I can't help but feel you now seem a bit more helpful."

Kelvin looked back into the den where the minister had started praying with his mother. "Seeing mom like this…it helps me to look at it as more than just a need for revenge—to catch whoever did this by any means necessary. I want it done properly, so the killer will see justice. And if I have to help the police in any way I can, I'm happy to do it."

"Forgive me for asking," Ava said, "but as one of the men of the house, can you just kindly ask the Duvalls to leave?"

Kelvin smiled and opened his mouth to speak. But before he could get a word out, another voice spoke up from down the hallway. It was Betty Duvall, and Ava quickly saw that Kelvin had not been exaggerating. The woman that had seemed almost relieved to see her husband handcuffed now looked absolutely livid.

"We will not leave because you arrested my husband for no good reason. This poor family is grieving the loss of their daughter and somehow, you saw fit to arrest one of their very best friends."

"Your husband charged at a detective and was showing insubordination during a murder investigation," Frank said.

"Do you have *any* idea what something like this could do to his reputation?"

Ava wasn't able to stop the words that came out of her mouth. They were simply too fast. "With all due respect, we're investigating the murder of a sixteen year-old girl. I don't give a damn about your husband's reputation."

James Duvall, the oldest son—the son that had been scheduled to marry Penny—slowly made his way to the argument. He looked tired and defeated, but there was enough spite in his voice to get his point across. "After my father talks to his lawyers about how he was treated, maybe you'll care then."

This seemed odd to Ava. James had been helpful before, even if it *had* been mostly because he'd let a family secret slip. The same went for Betty. She'd been resentful of her husband, quiet and clearly unhappy. She'd even looked somewhat happy to see a set of handcuffs placed around his wrists. She was like a totally different woman now and Ava couldn't help but wonder why. It was almost as if she and James were trying to do what they could to make themselves look like the victims here—not just the Picketts, a family that had just lost a daughter.

Ava saw that their bickering had disrupted the prayer in the den. Millie was looking at them with great sorrow and grief, while the minister looked understandably frustrated. She brushed by Betty Duvall and started down the hallway. Looking straight at Kelvin, she said, "Do you think now is a good time to speak to your father?"

"Yes." He was clearly also startled by the way Betty and James were reacting. When Betty opened her mouth to argue, he shot her a look that was tinged with ice and venom. Betty shut her mouth right away and looked into the den, resigned.

Ava and Frank made their way down to George Pickett's study again. Frank knocked on the already-opened door before they entered. "Mr. Pickett, do you think we could have a word with you?"

George was sitting behind his desk, partially collapsed into the large leather chair behind it. He looked up to them and it was clear that he had come here to have a moment to allow himself to break. His eyes were red, his face puffy. Though he appeared to be done with his emotional moment, it had certainly taken its toll on him.

"Yes, please, come in."

The detectives entered, Ava making sure to keep a few steps behind Frank. It was quite clear that people in this part of town (or, rather, perhaps just men accustomed to wealth and getting their way) did not take kindly to women taking the lead. She found it closed-minded and insulting but she also knew it was something she was just going to have to deal with if she hoped to have any success.

"It seems we angered some of your guests by arresting Mack Duvall," Frank said.

George chuckled and shrugged, as if he really didn't care. "I'm sure you were just doing your job."

"We were," Ava said. "But because of that and the freshness of what had happened when we first arrived, we never got to speak directly to you, one-on-one. We have to start with the simplest questions, of course: do you have *any* idea who might have done this?"

He shook his head slowly for several seconds. It reminded Ava of the pendulum of a clock. "No. I've been asking myself that very same question over and over again and come up with nothing." He looked to them both with tired chagrin and said, "But I can pretty much guarantee you it wasn't Mack. He's not the type."

"Speaking of Mack, there's one thing we need to discuss," Frank said. "We know that there was an argument about the marriage between Penny and James last night. Even Mack admitted it. Can you tell us why you were so quick to agree with Penny—that this plan you and the Duvalls had mapped out was suddenly up for discussion?"

There was a span of roughly five seconds where it appeared George was actually thinking about an answer. But then, without bothering to sit up in his chair, he fired off the same sort of indignation they'd received in the hall from Betty and James Duvall.

"That has absolutely nothing to do with what happened to Penny! That is a private, family matter that I will not allow to be scrutinized by the police."

"Mr. Pickett, you have to look beyond your friendships here," Ava said. "There was an argument *about* your daughter in your home last night, and this morning she is found dead. You can't just look past the coincidence of that."

Now he did sit up and when he did, he slammed a fist down on his desk. "It is absolutely preposterous to think that anyone in this family or among my guests would have done anything like this. It's abhorrent and offensive."

"But in that argument," Frank said, again injecting some bass into his voice, "you *did* take her side, right?"

"Yes, I did," he said right away. "A child is not like a business decision. I love my children and would give my life for them. Over the past year or so, I have watched Penny mature into this bright and capable young woman. She was exceptionally smart and…" he stopped here, taking in a large, hitching breath as he fought off a wave of tears. "And I would have stood by her decision. The argument last night was about that and nothing more."

Ava didn't buy it for a minute, thinking there was something more going on between Mack Duvall and George Pickett than was being revealed. "Mack said the two of you mended your fences this morning. No harm, no foul. Is that correct?"

George seemed surprised by this for a moment, but nodded all the same. "Yes. We've been friends for a very long time. You have an argument, you talk it out afterwards, and you move on. Now, instead of grilling me about friends and acquaintances, why don't you do me a favor and do your jobs? Start by telling me if there are any suspects or leads."

"None," Frank said. "But we are lo—"

"In that case, I'd like you to leave my home. We are all exhausted and, as I'm sure you can imagine, devastated."

This struck Ava as very odd. He wasn't even asking them to search the house over, to do whatever they needed to find any clues. Instead, it seemed like he was dismissing them altogether.

"Very well," Frank said. "We'll leave you to your sorrows. Thank you for your time, Mr. Pickett."

Ava looked to Frank, shocked. But he turned his head away just as she regarded him, already heading for the door. Ava took one last look back to George and nearly started asking him more questions despite Frank's decision to leave. In the end, though, she decided to trust Frank though, for the life of her, she could not understand why the hell he was giving into these people. She followed him out of the front door with a fresh batch of wails from Millie Pickett weaving through to usher them out.

CHAPTER NINE

"Just when I start warming up to you, it turns out you bow to the wealthy and stubborn."

The comment from Ava stung Frank, but he didn't let it show. He had to remind himself that despite her keen eye and attention to detail, she was still very new to this. She didn't know when to stop pushing and when to let something rest, when it was clear further pushing would only make things worse.

"I did not bow to anyone," he said. "That family is in the middle of grieving. As bothersome and irritating as they may be, losing a child is something that hurts in all classes of society. That deep in their grief, we wouldn't get much out of them. Staying any longer than we did would have been rude."

He could see that it helped to ease her anger a bit, but she was still fuming. He understood it. He usually left fuming anytime he had to speak more than two sentences to men with the stature of George Pickett and Mack Duvall.

"So what do we do now, then?" Ava demanded. "We have no leads, no clues, and two angry families…and we just breezed off. I don't get it."

"I know you don't," he said. "At the risk of sounding like a teacher here—which is the absolute *last* thing I want—it's all about trying to read the people you're dealing with. George Pickett was riding the line between being sad and being angry. Either side of that line he falls on, he's not going to be much help to us."

"You really buy that there was nothing more to that argument last night?"

"I honestly don't know. I do get the feeling that there's something fishy going on there. But if they want to chisel each other, that's none of my concern. I have to trust, though, that George meant what he said—that he'd do anything for his children. That leads me to believe that he'd let us know if there was something worth looking into, even if it did involve Mack Duvall."

"Okay, so I suppose I can buy that. But it takes me back to my original question. What do we do now?"

"Nothing. We both checked that room over. There was nothing."

"There was that smear of grease."

"That's true," Frank said, thoughtfully. "But it was nowhere else in the house and you said yourself that the windows did not look as if anyone had tried breaking in. The most we can do now is wait for the coroner's report…maybe see if there were any prints or telltale markings on the body."

Ava nodded. Frank could see something like embarrassment on her face. He wondered if she was beginning to feel very inexperienced. He figured that when she'd jumped into the role of detective, she had not counted on having to rely on her patience or to deal with doing nothing more than waiting while a killer was loose on the streets somewhere. He also felt pretty sure that Clarence had never entertained her with tales of sitting around the station, waiting on someone to call or update them while the hands of the police were literally tied.

"You okay, Gold? Seems like something's eating at you. I've noticed it ever since we stopped by to see your old man this morning."

He thought she looked to be on the verge of saying something but shook her head after a few seconds. "No. I'm fine."

They were about two blocks away from the station at that point and Frank didn't see the point in pushing any further. Just like with any criminal suspect, he knew better than to push too hard. Ava had some real talents, and the last thing he wanted to do was to unintentionally close her off.

Yet even as they neared the station, he noticed her looking to the sidewalk, deep in thought. He hated to see her like that, so clearly struggling. And on the heels of it was something else—something he was not quite ready to admit.

Lord help him, he thought he might be falling for her.

***

To get her mind off of the day's frustrations, Ava decided she would go home and shower, slip by her dad's favorite café and order some food to go, and then surprise him and Jeffrey at his apartment. Maybe putting smiles on their faces would make up for the anger and sorrow she'd been confronted with for the majority of the day. As she entered her apartment building, her mind slowly turned back to the immigrant that had been accosted on the street. While most cops and detectives would likely not consider it a crime, it certainly felt like one to her. She'd never had to experience the lifestyles and attitudes of the wealthy in any real way until today and as far as she was concerned,

42

they were almost like some different species. What was the point in belittling those less fortunate than you? What was the point of—

Her thoughts came to a screeching halt when she came to her door. The first thing she noticed was that her door was just barely opened. The lock did not seem busted and there were no clear signs that anyone had recently attempted to break in, but it was open all the same.

Sitting in front of the door was a wadded-up bundle of newspaper. It was obvious something was wrapped up inside and whatever it was appeared to be bleeding. Ava's mind went to the darkest of places first, fearing the mob had gotten to Jeffrey or her father. But even as she started to lift her foot towards the covered shape, she could see a portion of it sticking out of the back. Still, she had to see; she used the toe of her shoe to pull the curled paper down.

There was a very large, very dead rat inside the newspaper. It had been cut from neck to groin and its neck had been broken, its head nearly turned all the way around.

There seemed to be no message on the paper or the rat, though the morbid gift served as enough of a message, she supposed. It was a safe assumption that this, too, was from the mob. A dead rat. Really, did threats get any more obvious that that?

Ava kicked the rat and its wrappings to the side as she drew her gun. With her free hand, she pushed the door open. She stepped inside quickly, her gun drawn. Entering through the kitchen, she could not see where anything had been disturbed. It was far from tidy, but that was only because she did not keep a tidy kitchen. She found nothing out of sorts, nothing out of place.

It was more of the same in the living room. It was just a little messy because she'd not straightened up for several days. She stood in the center of the room and tried to get a feel for the place. It was hard to understand the feeling that came through her, but she was certain no one had been in here recently. She'd lived in this place for nearly six years now and knew the way it felt. Still, she continued her search. The hallway was empty, as was the bedroom. She did have a slight moment of panic when she thought of the small cigar box Clarence had always kept stashed in their closet. She opened the closet and pulled the box out from behind the pair of boots he would never wear again.

Seeing the boots, she nearly started crying. The grief came out of nowhere, like some big dumb whale breaking the surface of a raging sea. *He'll never put his feet in these again. They're only taking up space in this closet.*

She shoved the boots aside with a gasp of emotion and focused back on the box. She opened it and was relieved to find that it had not been touched. The seven hundred spare dollars Clarence had slowly been setting aside as an emergency fund was all there. She slid the cigar box back into the closet and then, after a bit of thought, went ahead and placed the boots back as well.

She sat there for a moment, gun still in hand, and tried to remain calm. She still felt quite certain this was nothing more than a message from the mob. She simply didn't understand why the dead rat hadn't been enough. Why also break into her apartment if they weren't going to steal anything or wreck the place?

To her surprise, it was Clarence's voice that spoke up in her head. It was level and very conversational, as if he were sitting on the edge of the bed behind her. *Because they want you to know they can do whatever they want. It's not enough to leave a grisly message like a dead rat at your door. They want you to know they've been into your apartment, into your life, into your private spaces.*

She was terribly afraid this was very much the case. And if that was true, how much longer could she keep it from Frank or anyone else on the force for that matter? But beyond those questions was another one: even if she *did* tell Minard or Frank, what could be done? This was the mob, after all, a group that had spent the last handful of years proving that they were basically untouchable. They had dirty cops and even some judges in their pockets, and their reach went far beyond simple laws and regulations.

Slowly, Ava got to her feet and took a small suitcase out of the closet. She took the time to pack up two outfits and then grabbed some pajamas and a change of clothes for Jeffrey. She figured they could just stay at her dad's place tonight. She'd figure something out tomorrow, hopefully.

She took a bundle of washrags out of the apartment with her and properly disposed of the dead rat in the waste basket at the end of her block. She walked along the dusk-tinged streets to her father's gym and couldn't help but feel as if she were being watched.

CHAPTER TEN

Ava got to the gym just as her father was locking the door. He glanced at her through the window with a smile. When he opened the door to let her in, she smelled a very strong smell—the scent of something that had been cleaned. A little *over*-cleaned from the smell of it. There was a hint of bleach and soap hanging in the air, just enough to make her recoil.

"Did you clean?" she asked as he closed and locked the door behind her.

"Hell no. That would be Jeffrey. When's the last time you saw me clean?"

"Good point. So…you have my son cleaning for you now?"

"Yes. But it's okay. I paid him. And he did a pretty good job."

"Where is he now?" she asked as they started walking through the back of the gym towards the rickety stairs that led to the second floor apartment her father had been calling home for the last ten years or so.

"He's upstairs, reading something for sch—um, Ava?"

"Yes?"

"Why are you carrying a suitcase?"

She'd honestly thought she'd be able to get all the way upstairs without him noticing. She loved her father dearly, but he was not exactly the most detail-oriented man. She sighed and stopped directly in front of the stairs.

"Because Jeffrey and I need to stay here tonight."

Roosevelt said nothing for several seconds, his face slowly inching towards a look of worry. "Is it the mob?"

"I think so, yes."

"What is it this time?"

Even as she started to answer him, she decided to leave out the part about her door being opened. Somehow, she was sure he'd find that more troublesome than the dead rat. And even as she told him about the rat, she found herself downplaying it, leaving out the bloody details.

"Ava, this is serious."

"I know, Dad. And I'm going to figure it out, somehow."

"Are you—"

"I really want to just head up to Jeffrey right now."

She could tell that it was killing him to just drop the matter but he managed to do so. He gave her a smile that was clearly forced and then gestured for her to continue up the stairs.

It had been at least six months since she'd last stepped foot in her father's apartment. It wasn't exactly messy, but there was no real order to anything. It wasn't too bad of a place, so long as you could get over the fact that it was sitting over a boxing gym. The floors were very creaky, the single window looking out onto the street was in desperate need of a washing, and the hallway was thin, but it wasn't awful. She found Jeffrey sitting in the old chair her father sometimes dubbed "the throne," reading from his grammar textbook.

"Hey, Mom," he said, barely looking up from his book.

"Hey, kiddo I hear Grandpa put you to work."

"Yeah," he said with a hurtful tone. "Cleaning. But he paid me a whole quarter!"

"That's the way to do it! With that sort of pay, maybe I should quit the police and come work for Grandpa, what do you think?"

"No way in hell!" Roosevelt said as he made his way into the small, cramped kitchen. "A gym is no place for a dame!"

"I'm not a dame, I'm your daughter."

Roosevelt growled at her and then shot Jeffrey a look that seemed to say: *Can you believe this?*

This comic moment set the tone for the rest of the evening. It seemed to even salvage it when Jeffrey appeared less than thrilled that they'd have to stay over for the night. Roosevelt willingly gave up the bedroom, stating he would sleep in the throne. Ava knew it would mess his back up but said nothing; he was making a big deal about being excited over it as a way to get Jeffrey to not feel bad about displacing his grandfather.

It was nice to have dinner in her father's small kitchen. In the face of the luxuries and wealthy families she'd encountered today, it was comforting to be back in a place so small and close to her heart. Plus, it seemed to make her father incredibly proud to be hosting them for once and not the other way around. Dinner was occupied with typical small talk, mostly talking to Jeffrey about school and his friends. Ava could tell that her dad was still a little uneasy about the revelations she'd made about the mob. It seemed he was on the verge of bringing it up a few times during dinner but opted to keep it quiet around Jeffrey.

After dinner, she helped Jeffrey get ready for bed. He'd come more and more around to the idea of staying here for the night and by the time he was in his grandpa's bed, under the sheets, he seemed very comfortable. He went to sleep without an issue, without a complaint. When Ava ventured back out into the little living room space, she found her father sitting in the throne, working at the laces on an old pair of boxing gloves.

"Thanks again for this," she said, sitting down in the only other chair in the room—a small kitchen chair.

"Sure. You need to stay a few days longer?"

"I don't think so." She waited a moment and when the ridicule and questions she was expecting did not come, she gave her father a curious look. "You think I've gotten in over my head, don't you?"

"Not at all. I do think you might have jumped into a very deep lake without any real idea of how to swim, though. Aside from this whole mob thing…what else is going on? There's a lot of weight on your shoulders. I'm not the smartest man—just an old, bruised up Bruno— but even I can see that."

"You're plenty smart, Dad. And yes…today, there was this case. A murder but up on Fifth Avenue. Somehow, dealing with rich people was worse than dealing with the murder and that's got me all mixed up. The whole mob thing is just an added trouble. It feels like too much but it's also sort of motivating."

"That's because you're a fighter. You've never been one to back down, to give up. Having to raise you by myself, I always tried to bring you up so you'd never feel left out or less than in this world that is run by men." He set the boxing glove aside and seem to think hard about something for a moment. "So, being that father, I feel that I need to tell you not to back down. But at the same time, we're talking about the mob…so just make sure you're careful. Don't think you can take on the world by yourself when you have an entire police force to help you."

Ava nodded and they fell into silence. She was rather surprised; she'd fully expected him to tell her to get as far away from this career of hers as she could—that she'd made a mistake and it might not be too late to get out of it. She watched him work idly on the boxing glove and her thoughts turned elsewhere. She began to think of Clarence and how she'd not yet done much to really dig into the case of his murder. She'd not had the chance, honestly, and no one had ever brought it up to her. The little bit she *had* looked into it had been in secret and very quick. She thought she had enough to go on in order to start looking, but…

"Hey, Dad. You okay if I head out later? Maybe just go for a walk to clear my head?"

"Seems like that might be a bit dangerous, given all that you're going through."

"I'm a detective now, Dad. I know the safe parts to stick to."

He shrugged, keeping his attention on the laces which he'd nearly gotten untangled and back to form. "You're a grown woman," he said. "*And* a detective. You're fully capable of making your own decisions. I may be asleep when you come in, though."

"Okay. I'm going to make sure Jeffrey is fast asleep before I go anywhere, though. And you're sure you're good in your throne?"

He grinned and said, "I've spent many a night sleeping in this chair. It won't be anything new."

With that, Ava got to her feet, kissed her father on the head and started back for the bedroom.

"Hey, Ava?"

She turned to him and saw that he was smiling. "Yeah?"

"I'm proud of you. Just…stay safe."

"I will."

When she turned back around and headed down the hall, she could feel her father's eyes on her, caring and comforting.

***

While Ava had come mostly clean with the mob business, there was another secret she was keeping. Ava had one more secret she'd been holding on to for about ten days now, something she would not *dare* tell Frank. As far as she was concerned, she was doing nothing wrong but she was sticking her nose where it didn't quite belong.

She thought of this secret as she watched Jeffrey sleeping, the gentle rise and fall of his chest like her own beating heart. She went to her purse and pulled out the sheet of paper she'd folded and placed inside ten days ago. As she unfolded it, she could easily recall the woman she'd been speaking to when she took the notes written on the paper. The woman's name was Gloria Richland and she'd been confined to a hospital bed when Ava went to meet her. Beyond that meeting with Gloria Richland, though, there was something else—a conversation she'd overheard outside of Captain Minard's office shortly after she and Frank had closed their first case. Staring at the sheet of paper, she called the conversation to memory.

Minard's voice, coming through his door as he spoke to another officer: "*That description sounds too damned familiar to me. One more time. What did the witness see?*"

"*A man in a workman's coat,*" the other officer said. "*Sort of short. Fired four shots and took off with a woman's purse.*"

48

"And the woman? I assume she's dead?"

"Not as of half an hour ago. She's barely hanging on in the hospital."

That was the only snippet of the conversation she'd heard but it had been enough. Even after receiving a threatening note from an anonymous officer, that conversation had stuck with her. The description of the criminal was exactly the same as the man that had killed Clarence during what had, at first, sounded like nothing more than a simple robbery.

Ava had waited until later in the afternoon and picked up the name of the woman who had been shot through casual conversation down in the Women's Bureau offices. Frances had heard about it and was tasked with filing the report when asked to interview Gloria Richland. Ava waited another day, when Frances had already spoken with Gloria, to make a visit of her own.

She read over the notes she'd taken during her own secret interview as she sat on the floor of the small bedroom.

A man of small stature, but with shoulders like bookshelves. A driver's cap that looked almost silly. Not sure, but sounded like he had some sort of speech impediment. All he said to her was: "Give me than damned purse or I'll be taking a hell of a lot more from you." And then he shot anyway. Three of his four shots landed—one in the chest, two in the leg.

Gloria will pull through but, at the age of 37, may always walk with a cane.

Ava put the paper back into her purse and checked on Jeffrey. He was dead to the world and, much like his father, would be pretty much impossible to wake up at this point. She kissed him on the cheek and headed out, thinking of Gloria Richland and the short-statured man that had robbed her and then tried to kill her—a man she now believed could very well be the same man that took Clarence from her.

She knew better than to go looking for someone like Tony Two, hoping he might provide some information. If she willingly *went* to the mob, that might be the end of her career—or even her life. Besides, there was no way in hell he would offer to help her after what she'd done to him during the hatchet-killer case.

That meant the only place she could expect any hope of answers would be the same places that had gotten the ball rolling on the hatchet-killer case. She was going to have to go back to the Key Factory and ask around. Jack Dooley liked to pretend that he kept his hands clean, but running a small jazz club that also dealt on the speakeasy scene, he couldn't help but get those hands dirty from time to time. Besides that, Jack had always liked her and was a loyal friend—which he'd showed in spades the last time she spoke with him.

With that in mind, she left her father's apartment and hailed a cab. It was a ten-minute drive down to the Key Factory and she was surprised to find that she still got excited at the thought of going inside. She'd performed there as a ruse to get the hatchet-killer to come out of the shadows just several days ago and, even though it had not gone down as planned, it had still been a pivotal moment in her life. It had showed her that she did still have some of that magic that spun itself around any performer on a stage. She had missed it during the time she'd spent away from such clubs and it was encouraging to know she still had it.

Of course, there would be no performing tonight. As she watched the streets and buildings pass by through the cab windows, she tried to figure out just how much to ask. She did not want to get Jack Dooley in trouble with the mob or even lowlife criminals like the man she was currently investigating. She figured she should keep the questions to a minimum and not give any hard information.

When the cab dropped her off, she could hear the bass notes and trumpet of a song she was not familiar with. When she stepped inside, she saw a small crowd and a simple little jazz trip up on the stage. There were only about twenty or so people in attendance, bobbing their heads in a haze of smoke and sweat. Because the crowd was so small, she had no problem spotting Jack. He was sitting at a table over near the counter, speaking animatedly to an attractive young woman. Ava made her way over to him, again amazed at how something as simple as the thrumming of a bassline could help to settle her heart. She almost hated to interrupt Jack because he seemed quite enamored with the young lady he was speaking to. But when he saw her coming, he seemed not to mind. He said one last thing to the woman before excusing her politely. The woman got up, nodded to Ava as she passed, and ventured off to another seat.

"Ava Gold, what can I do for you, sweetie?" Jack asked.

"Hey, Jack." She nodded up to the stage and said, "They aren't too bad."

"Glad you think so. All three are pretty new to the scene. They asked if they could come up on the stage tonight and just sort of riff. I think I might have them back sometime soon." He grinned and said, "Is that why you're here? Want to lead another set?"

"No, not yet. Maybe some other time, though. But for now…I was hoping you could maybe help me out. I'm looking for information on a certain man. I don't have a name and not a very good description. But I know you get all kinds in here *and* that you tend to hear murmurings from some of the seedier crowds."

"Ah, so you want me to be a pigeon."

"I suppose that's one way to put it."

He smiled, though it was clear he was a bit nervous. "The way I hear it, the last time I gave you some information, it ended up with you arresting a mob associate that was released pretty quickly afterwards."

"That's true. But then I came in here and performed a few nights later and blew the roof off the place. I'd say that makes us even."

"Would a similar trade be in the cards if I help you out?"

Ava enjoyed the back and forth banter but felt that it might be getting a little too light-hearted. "Let's see if you can help first. I'm looking for a man that is probably a little on the short side, but with a decent build. He has something of a speech impediment and wears a driver's cap of some kind."

"Well, the driver's cap thing isn't much help because those stupid-looking things are everywhere." He thought for a second and then slowly started to shake his head. "Nothing like that is ringing any bells. And let's face it…someone with a speech impediment is going to get a nickname in a place like this. You think this guy is another mobster?"

"Doubtful. I'm thinking more a small-time thing. Purse-snatching, things like that." She thought, but did not say, *and murdering my husband.*

"I can't think of anything off the top of my head," Jack said, "but I can ask around."

"No, don't ask. Don't stir up any suspicion. Maybe just listen extra closely and keep your eyes open."

"Short guy with a dumb hat and a speech impediment."

"That's right," she said, rather disappointed that she'd come up empty handed. "Thanks, Jack."

She got up to leave, but Jack reached out and took her hand. "Why the rush? Stay a while and listen!"

That was all the convincing Ava needed. It felt good to just sit there and watch three musicians playing, welding their craft on stage. She could tell that the trumpeter was still learning, but he was insanely good all the same. Before long, Ava was bobbing her head right along with the other patrons and for even the smallest little fraction of time, all of her burdens slipped away—including the fact that she was right back to zero   with   finding   Clarence's   killer.

CHAPTER ELEVEN

When Ava arrived at work the following morning, Frank was waiting for her near the front desk. He had an annoyed look on his face and when he saw her, he waved her over.

"You don't look happy," Ava said.

"That's because I'm not happy. Minard wants to see us. I asked what it was about and he refused to tell me. He wanted both of us to be present."

"That can't be good, can it?"

He frowned and shrugged, trying to play it off even though Ava could tell that he was nervous. There was a moment when Ava was worried that maybe Minard had somehow found out about her late-night escapades the night before. She *knew* that was very unlikely but the worry was there all the same.

They crossed the bullpen and came to Minard's office, where Frank knocked on the door. Minard barked for them to come in and Frank wasted no time opening the door. Upon entering, Ava closed it. She could already tell just by the look on Captain Minard's face that her hunch was correct: this was not going to be a good-news sort of meeting.

"Sit," Minard said gruffly, pointing to the chairs in front of his desk.

They did, Ava a little slower than Frank. While Frank was quick to obey pretty much anything Minard barked his way, Ava was genuinely confused as to why he would be angry with them. Then, just as she thought she might have an answer, Minard started speaking and confirmed it. just as it came to her mind.

"Betty and Mack Duvall had filed a complaint against the two of you," he said. "They're demanding apologies."

"Well of course they'd file a complaint," Ava said. "I arrested Mack."

"Yes, that's part of it. But they claim it was unprompted."

"He charged me, sir," Ava said. "Not only that, but he was being very difficult when we were trying to ask questions and get more information about what happened to Penny Pickett."

"You understand we had to let him go, though," Minard said.

"So was I wrong to arrest him?"

Minard thought about it for a moment before answering. "Maybe. Maybe you could have handled it differently. Whatever the case, you need to offer that whole family an apology—and likely the Picketts as well."

"Sir," Frank said, "that's a little much. Don't you think it's nothing more than a rich family that isn't used to being treated like the common man?"

"That's not for me to decide."

"With all due respect," Ava said, "it's *exactly* for you to decide."

"Watch your tone, Gold," Minard said.

She chewed on her next question before finally speaking it. "Would you have taken this bunk as seriously if it had come from any plain old guy off the streets?"

She saw a flicker of annoyance in the Captain's face and she knew she'd hit a nerve. "Probably not," he admitted. "And you know what…if there weren't a dead sixteen year-old girl wrapped up in all of this, I may have waved it off. But the fact remains that your arrest of Mack Duvall makes it seem like this case is more about proving a point to the wealthy than anything else." He then looked to Frank and said: "The same goes for you. You could have stopped her. Instead, the Duvalls say you were in full support of her."

"I was. He was being belligerent and difficult. Plus, like she said, he charged her. If he'd charged me, I would have done the same thing."

Minard steepled his fingers and leaned forward across his desk. "You want me to come out and say it? Fine? Treat these rich assholes with kid's gloves. The last thing we need is for a group of wealthy citizens to start railing against the police. Keep that in mind today as you go out and find this girl's killer." There was an awkward pause between the three of them, which Minard ended by gently slapping his desk. "Get out there, already."

Ava was the one fast to respond this time, mainly because she wanted to be out of his office. She had already opened the door and stepped out of it before Frank had made it all the way out of his chair. He caught up to her halfway across the bullpen and gently took her by the arm, doing his best not to draw attention to themselves.

"Come on, Gold. Did you really think we were going to get away with arresting Mack Duvall? If you ask me, that moment in there with Minard just now was no worse than a simple slap on the wrist."

"I agree. But it wasn't warranted. Did you not hear the part where the captain of the police force instructed us to treat the wealthy differently than we would anyone else?"

"I did. And no, I did not appreciate it."

They passed through the bullpen and lobby, out into the morning. It wasn't quite chilly, but the heat of summer had long ago packed it in. Ava started to walk in the direction of Fifth Avenue, her feet already aching from the thought of the rather lengthy walk.

"No walking today," Frank said. "Didn't you hear? We've moved up in the world."

"How's that?"

"As of this morning, at least one policeman per squad and every detective has access to an automobile. There's about a dozen Ford flatheads parked in the back lot. I filled out the form this morning. You and I are scheduled to use one for the next week."

She couldn't contain her smile, which was saying a lot since she was still riled up from the meeting with Minard. "My feet thank you," she said.

As they headed to the rear lot, the sudden presence of a car in their line of duty slowly started to make a lot of sense. Maybe *that* was why Minard was so worried about angering wealthy citizens. Maybe there were ultra-wealthy people that had some sort of say in how much financing went into the police department. And if word got out that those with deep pockets were being harassed by the police in any way, extravagances such as Ford flatheads would be harder to come by.

The thought triggered another thought in her head as they approached their car. Frank opened the door for her and she nodded her appreciation as she slid into the front seat. She kept thinking about how quickly George Pickett had disagreed with Mack Duvall when it had come to his daughter. If it had been that easy for him to lose it on Duvall—one wealthy man to another—surely there had been other hiccups in their relationship. They were, after all, businessmen that ran and operated successful businesses and factories. If there was some sort of merger on the horizon for them, she didn't see how they would *never* have an argument.

"Hey, do you know where George Pickett's workplace is?" she asked.

"Vaguely," Frank said as he slid behind the wheel. "I don't even know the name, really, but it's the rubber factory over in midtown. He's doing so damned well for himself because these things," he said, tapping on the car's steering wheel, "are only going to be in more and more demand. And with tires…" He made a whistling noise to finish the sentence, as if he could not comprehend the amount of money the man stood to make in the coming years.

Ava grinned when she saw how comfortable and happy Frank looked as he slid the key into the ignition. The car did not look brand new; she supposed it could have been a model automobile from a dealership elsewhere in town—the example that dealers would let interested buyers test out.

"I think we should head over there," she said. "Ask around to see if we're getting the entire picture of what's going on between the Picketts and Duvalls."

"I have to admit, that's a good idea. But if Pickett finds out…"

"Then Minard can slap my wrist again."

"My wrist is being slapped, too, you know?"

"Well, we'll say we were allowing the family time to grieve…waiting for the Duvalls to cool down from yesterday's unfortunate events. We thought it would be prudent to look elsewhere."

Frank started backing out of the parking spot, and she was glad to see he had some experience. She could tell by the way he wasn't going all rigid and stiff behind the wheel. She'd only driven a car once and she'd nearly crashed the damned thing.

"Yeah, that's plausible," he said. "Let's head over there. And if we do get called in for wrist-slapping, you recite everything you just said."

He pulled the car out onto the streets and Ava, who was really only accustomed to riding in cabs, thought it was rather surreal. Automobiles weren't new to the police force, but they weren't a *staple*. Not yet, anyway. But they were quickly becoming more and more normalized—just another way this world was moving on in a hurry, anxious to grow into something bigger. And, in the case of sixteen year-old Penny Pickett, a hell of a whole lot meaner.

CHAPTER TWELVE

The factory, which was called, rather unoriginally, Pickett Rubber, was a rather average-looking building. Anyone that happened to just take a single look at the building from the outside would never guess that it was run by a millionaire. Ava and Frank quickly discovered that the interior wasn't much better. Walking in through the front door, they entered a small lobby that, while decorated moderately well, still smelled of the rubber being processed and manufactured on the other side of the wall.

A very busy-looking man sat behind a table, smoking a cigarette and furiously scribbling numbers down onto a legal pad. He looked up to Ava and Frank with a tired expression on his face.

"I'll be right with you," the man said. "Just a little busy today, that's all."

"No worries at all," Ava said, taking advantage of the man's obvious troubles with whatever he was writing down. She showed her ID while Frank, following suit, flashed his badge. "We're with the NYPD and just needed to have a look around on the floor. Do we need to have that cleared with anyone?"

"Not really," the man said, barely looking up from his pad and puffing away on his smoke. "Maybe the foreman. His name is Cal Nettle. He's out there somewhere." He waved idly to the right and said, "The first big door on your left. Help yourselves."

They exited the lobby down the small hallway the man had indicated. Through the large metal door, they entered into the only other space in the building—a huge, open-floored warehouse. There were several machines sitting in the center of the room, some connected with odd-looking belts that were held up by steel rods. Ava watched as one of these conveyor belts carried a chunk of rectangular rubber to its neighboring machine. This machine, from what Ava could tell, was to cut the rubber into different lengths. From there, two men were hauling the rubber away on wheeled crates.

It all happened very quickly, leaving Ava to notice an overall distressing thing about the factory. As the realization settled in, Frank seemed to read her mind and vocalized her exact thoughts.

"This place is a shithole," he chuckled.

He was right. While the work itself and the way the men performed it was quite impressive, the factory was a wreck. The floors were covered in chunks of rubber, dirt, grime, and portions of crates that seemed to have broken. There were shelves in the back, but it looked like a location where a child had thrown its toys out of disinterest. Everything was cluttered and Ava couldn't imagine how anyone found what they were looking for among the mess.

As for the workers, some of them looked to be no older than thirteen. The smaller ones were working just as hard, if not harder, than the older and more experienced ones. Something about it tugged fiercely at Ava's heart.

As she and Frank took the place in, a large man with dirt and dust covering most of his face came over to them. When he used a handkerchief to wipe most of it away, he revealed a face with some age to it. Ava guessed him to be in his mid-to-late fifties.

"Can I help you folks?"

Frank showed his badge, which he had never put away after showing the man in the lobby. "Detectives Wimbly and Gold, NYPD."

The older gentleman regarded Ava as if he'd never seen a woman before—which was fair, because she supposed he'd never seen a woman *detective.* She smiled, as if to let him know she got that reaction all the time.

He offered his hand to both of them, seeming a little reluctant to do so when he offered it to Ava for a shake. "I'm Cal Nettle. I'm the foreman for the day shift. Is there something I can do for you folks?"

"We're just trying to get a feel for what it's like to work here," Ava said, raising her voice to be heard over the sounds of the machines and squeaking wheels and belts.

"This is about Mr. Pickett's daughter, isn't it?" Cal asked.

"It's part of the investigation, yes," Frank said.

"Mr. Nettle, do you enjoy working here?" Ava asked.

"Most of the time, sure. It's a steady paycheck, and I'm not stupid enough to take that for granted. Some people would give anything for steady paycheck these days."

"And is Mr. Pickett a good boss?"

"Well, he's rarely here. We see him maybe two or three times a month. But when he does show up, he's pleasant enough."

"What about Mack Duvall? He ever come around?"

"Who's that now?" Cal asked.

It was answer enough for Ava. Honestly, it came as no surprise. If George Pickett barely spent time in this factory that earned him millions a year, why would Mack Duvall bother showing up?

"What about Mr. Pickett's family?" Frank asked, moving right along. "What do you know about them? He ever talk about them?"

"Well, I can't be help much there, either. The only member of his family I ever saw or even talked to was little Penny. Damn shame what happened to her. That girl sure was a treasure."

"You knew her?"

"Fairly well I suppose. She came in just about every time her father showed his face in here. She seemed very interested in the machines and how everything was run. She was smart, you know? Always asking questions. And if she thought your answer was lacking, boy would she ever tell you!"

"What do you mean?" Ava asked.

"That girl paid attention," Cal said. "Two visits here and she knew just about everything there was to know. The last few times she was in here, she was coming to me and making suggestions about how we could do things better. And you know what? We didn't take any of her suggestions, but they all made sense."

I wonder if one of those suggestions was to clean up a bit, Ava wondered. But beyond that, she had another thought forming. And though it made no real sense, she thought it might be worth pursuing.

"What about Kelvin?" she asked. "Did he ever come in?"

"He did, but it's been a while. He's older, of course. Got married and lives in another town somewhere close by, I think."

Frank apparently caught on to where Ava was headed because his follow-up question was on the tip of Ava's tongue. "Has he ever worked here in any capacity?"

"If he did, I was unaware of it. He used to come in when he was a kid, just like Penny did. Now, rumor has it that Kelvin has some sort of stake in the place so I'm sure he'll end up getting involved in *some* capacity. But for now...I just don't know for sure." He looked to the floor and sighed deeply at something. He quickly turned back to Ava and Frank with a frown on his face. "Unless there's something else really important, I need to get back out there. George may not have been here physically but whenever he's away for an extended period of time, the place sort of falls apart without him checking in."

"That's perfectly fine," Frank said. "Thank you for your time, Mr. Nettle."

They watched as he hurried out onto the floor, sidestepping an old, discarded piece of rubber and starting to yell at one of the younger workers.

"Seems strange, doesn't it?" Frank said.

"Well, on the surface, it seems sort of sweet. I know it's a little odd for a father to be more involved with his daughter's life than his older son, but yes…it's strange. Maybe George Pickett will be able to shed some light on it for us."

"Or maybe we'll get another complaint filed against us," Frank countered.

"Maybe," she said. "What do you say we go find out?"

CHAPTER THIRTEEN

Ava was not prone to thoughts of grandeur or self-importance but even she had to admit that it felt a bit more fitting to pull up in front of the Picketts' Fifth Avenue home in a fairly new Ford flathead. Even then, though, as she and Frank stepped out, she couldn't help but feel out of place. They walked to the door side by side and after knocking, were greeted by Evelyn.

"Hey there," Evelyn said. She sounded uncertain, as if she were surprised that they'd even bothered coming by again. She kept any additional comments to herself, though. She simply opened the door wider and let them in.

"Are Mr. and Mrs. Pickett home?" Ava asked.

"Yes ma'am. Mr. Pickett is in his study and Mrs. Pickett is up in Penny's room. She went in there yesterday evening and hasn't come out yet. I tried taking her food two different times, but she won't eat."

"And what about the Duvalls?" Frank asked. "Are they here as well?"

"No, sir. They left last night and I haven't heard or seen from them since." She looked to the floor, chewing at her lip. It was clear to Ava that she was holding back something.

"Is something wrong, Evelyn?"

"I know I have no right to say such a thing, but I don't know that it's a good idea that you're here. They're still pretty mad about what happened yesterday."

"That's understandable," Frank said. "But we have a job to do. And if they want to find out what happened to their daughter, we need to be able to do that job. And sometimes it means asking hard questions in difficult times."

Ava thought it was well said and took it as their cue to head across the foyer and down the hallway to George's office. The office door was open, but Frank knocked before stepping in. George was sitting behind his desk, his head propped up in his right hand as he scanned several sheets of paper. He looked up at the sound of knocking and fumed when he saw the detective standing there.

"No," he said. "Get out."

"Sir," Ava said. "We're only trying to—"

"Haven't you done enough?" George yelled, getting to his feet. "Do you know the sort of circus I'm having to put up with after you hauled Mack out of here yesterday?"

"I don't give a damn about Mack Duvall," Ava said. "All I'm concerned with is trying to find out who killed your daughter. And quite frankly, it baffles me that you seem not to want that help."

"How dare you even *suggest* that I—"

"We paid a visit to your rubber factory," Frank interrupted. "Had a talk with the day shift foreman."

"Ah, so you're taking this into my work now, are you?"

Ava stepped into the room, doing her best to keep her voice calm. "Sir, this is how police investigations work. We ask questions. Very hard ones at times. I can't imagine the pain of losing a child. I have a young son and if he were taken from me, I imagine I'd be just as out of my mind as you are at the moment. But I assure you, we are only trying to help."

George sighed and collapsed back into his chair. He eyed them both skeptically. "So why bother going to the factory?"

"To get a better idea of what your business looks like," Ava said. "With a future merger between you and Mack Duvall, we were curious about the workers, the environment, and all of that."

"And what, exactly, does that have to do with Penny's murder?"

"You said you and George rarely fought. The sudden disagreement over the marriage of your children made us wonder if there may have been something you weren't telling us."

"That's nearly an invasion of my privacy!"

"No, sir," Frank said. "That's called police work."

"Besides," Ava said, getting a word in before George could have another little outburst. "Nothing came up. What we *did* discover was that Penny was something of a regular at the factory. The foreman said she really enjoyed visiting the place."

"She did," George said, and it was the first time Ava had seen him smile. It was brief and sad, but it was a smile all the same. "Penny was exceptionally bright. She'd often hear me talking about issues at work while we were at the dinner table and quickly gave me her suggestions. She was very interested in what I do. She knew we were wealthy, but never took it for granted; it was like she wanted to know where all the money came from and when she found out, she was *very* interested in taking part."

"Did she ever actually *work* there or just sort of stayed behind the scenes?"

George laughed for a second and Ava was surprised to find that it was a rather joyous sound. "Oh, she begged and begged me to let her work there. But you were there this morning, so you saw it…it's just no place for a young lady. So I told her that when she was done with school and had settled down with a husband and started a family, I'd find her some sort of administrative job. She seemed excited about it and, to tell you the truth, I was already thinking about a job much higher than that. Something on the board of directors, perhaps. She and I had brief discussions about her eventually buying out the Duvalls much later on."

"Did you keep this from the Duvalls?" Frank asked.

"Not at all. It was no secret—if we waited several years, everyone stood to make a great deal of money." He stopped for a moment, considering. "It's one of the reasons I was so quick to take Penny's side when she decided she wanted out of the marriage. The one thing Penny and I *had* kept secret was that if we could figure out a way to buy Mack out by the time she was eighteen, then the marriage wouldn't even have to happen."

It did not escape Ava that when George was given the opportunity to talk about his daughter, he did so with great excitement and joy. As he'd spoken during the past two minutes, it was almost as if the mention and memory of his daughter had made him forget that he was upset with them. But as he dived deeper and deeper into the inner workings of this multi-layered merger plan, she doubted they'd get much more. Already, each word he spoke seemed to be coming with more and more hesitancy.

"Did Kelvin ever show any interest in the family business?"

"No. But I suppose that's because I pretty much forced it on him. He worked the floor when he was fifteen but clearly hated it. He was more interested in the business side of things but he just….well, he's always been a well-behaved child but he just doesn't have the mind or the personality for business. And because we *do* have wealth, I understood we had the ability to allow our children to do whatever they pleased when it came to their future. I believe Kelvin has his eye on being an educator or a—"

He stopped abruptly and then shook his head. Massaging his forehead as if to stave off a headache, he sat back in the chair, so crumpled into it that Ava thought he might fall out.

"Mr. Pickett?"

"None of this has anything to do with Penny's death. And I'm actually very hurt that you'd go so deep into these things. Shouldn't you be out there on the streets, looking for her killer?"

"Yes," Ava said. "But finding clues of where to start begin here, at home. And so far, we have nothing."

"Well maybe you need to work *harder*," George said, sitting up and shouting so suddenly that Ava found herself taking a step back.

Ava raised her hands gently in front of her and nodded. "Fine. Thank you for your time."

She saw that Frank look confused, like he wanted to stay to see what else they could get out of him. But Ava thought they may have actually gotten more than either of them realized as they stood in the office. She gave him a brief nod, indicating she indeed thought it was time to go.

"We'll leave you now," Frank said. "But please…I know there were lots of people in and out of here over the past few days. If you can think of *anything* that seemed remotely strange or out of the ordinary, call the station and ask for either of us."

George nodded but also waved them away as if they were nothing more than pesky flies. It had Ava making her exit and starting to feel quite confident that George Pickett was being so difficult because he didn't want this case solved at all.

They left the house together and headed back out on the street where a very fine mist of rain had started to fall. They slid into the Ford and as Frank started the engine, he gave Ava a slightly annoyed look.

"So are you going to let me know what you're thinking, or should I start guessing?" Frank said as he started up the Ford.

"I think we looked right over Kelvin Pickett just because he doesn't live at home."

"Well, he was at his own home the morning the body was discovered."

"True. But George just offered up a little nugget, didn't he? He said that Penny was the one he was leaning more towards in terms of handing over most of the business. Of course, he did not come out and say it, but if he was going to have her come on board and buy out the Duvall portion after the merger, I think that paints the picture."

Pulling out into traffic, Frank thought this over for a moment. "But he said Kelvin didn't seem to really care for it."

"No, he said Kelvin was only interested in the business side of it. He didn't want to work that dirty floor. He wanted to be in the boardrooms and banks. So if he found out that there was a plan in motion to set Penny on that course, maybe he felt slighted."

"Slighted enough to kill his sister?" he asked, doubtful. "If anything, I'm maybe eyeing Mack Duvall a little harder. If he somehow found out about the Picketts' plan to end the marriage after the buyout, that could have upset him. It could have made him feel like a pawn."

"He'd be getting a payday either way, though," Ava pointed out.

"I do have to admit that your theory has some weight. To be the oldest child—a *son* at that—and have the business power of the family go to your *sister*…I suppose that would be something of a slap in the face."

"Not to mention if his plan in academia didn't work out and he had to come back to the factory, he'd be working with a woman as his supervisor. Even if it *was* a family member, he'd never outlive that."

"It fits," Frank said, "but I don't know. Kelvin seemed just as wrecked over his sister's death."

"Of course he did. Let's say, just for fun, that he did it. That he's the killer, isn't he going to do his absolute best to make it seem like he's terribly upset?"

"Yes. But…remember what Minard said."

"Oh, I remember. Give these rich people special treatment for no other reason than them being rich."

"I don't think he put it quite like that," Frank said. "Okay, Gold. Tell me…what do you think our next move is here?"

She waited a moment before answering, unsure if he was truly asking for her opinion or if it was some sort of test. "Well, I think the would-be husband is still worth looking into—if not as a suspect, then as a potential source of information. But I do also strongly think we need to speak to Kelvin."

"I don't know that Mack Duvall is going to let you anywhere *near* his home. Or his son, for that matter."

"So we split up," Ava said. "You go visit the Duvalls. Maybe without a woman present, Mack will be more forthcoming."

"And you're going to head Wyatt River to speak with Kelvin?"

"Sure. I think as long as his father or the Duvalls aren't around, he'll talk. Even if it's not much…we really just need to see if we can back up George's story. But if he happens to offer up more, that's even better."

"I think that's a smart play," Frank said. "But I'm not so sure about letting you go off on your own. Not after yesterday."

"Damn it, Frank! You said yourself you would have done the same thing if Mack Duvall had come charging after you. What else was I supposed to do? Look…I know I'm going to sound like some wacko dame but so be it. But while you and I are working on something like this, you need to decide if you're more worried about working together with your partner, or making sure you appeal to every little sidelong glance Minard might give us."

"Fine," he conceded. "But *you're* going to also have to understand that, like it or not, the vast majority of this town isn't ready to accept the idea of a woman detective. That means every move you make is being scrutinized and studied. You *have* to be careful…you have to be smart about everything you do."

"I'm aware of that," she said, slowly swallowing down some of her anger.

"So if we do split up like you're suggesting, please try to play nice. Don't push too hard on Kelvin Pickett. Any time you get in trouble with Minard, it looks bad on me, too."

She couldn't stand that he was pushing on her, stressing over what Minard might think. While she did understand that her fledgling career rested in Minard's hands, she also didn't see the point in being a detective if she was going to be constantly restrained by a constantly overbearing supervisor.

"I appreciate the concern, Frank, but I don't need a babysitter."

He scowled at her, shaking his head. "What's going on with you?"

"Nothing. I'm fine."

"No, you're lying. Ever since you chose to swing by your dad's gym yesterday, there's been something off about you. And if there *is* something going on, I feel like you need to tell me. At the risk of once again coming off as an instructor, I can tell you that when personal stuff is weighing heavy on your mind, it can end up interfering far too much wit—"

"I'm fine," she said, raising her voice this time. "Now, if you'll let me out here, I'll catch a cab to Wyatt River. It's only…what? Maybe twenty minutes or so out of the city?"

She hated that she'd snapped at him, but she didn't need him digging around in her personal life while they were working to find Penny Pickett's killer. It also made her want to eventually share her troubles with him less and less.

"Yeah, let's do that," he said absently. "Just do what you can to be back at the station by five. I have a feeling Captain Minard is going to want an update." He glared ahead and pointed and when he did, she thought he looked almost sad. "There's a cab. Want to hop out and get it?"

Ava didn't say a single word when she got out. She barely even looked in Frank's direction as he pulled to the side of the road to let her out. Stepping out of the car, she instantly started waving down the cab on the other side of the street. Rushing over to it, she felt an immense relief to be away from Frank—and she hated it.

CHAPTER FOURTEEN

Kelvin Pickett's home was nowhere near as regal as the one his parents owned, but it was still quite impressive, given that Kelvin was only nineteen years old. The house still managed to stand out as somewhat classier than the other homes in Wyatt River; it was a new two-story build in an area of the small town that appeared to be in a constant state of new development. The columns on the front porch and the sparkling windows seemed to shadow the influence of his parents just twenty or so minutes away.

Ava had decided somewhere between getting in the cab and being dropped off that she wasn't going to just go up to the door and knock. While Kelvin hadn't been particularly problematic yesterday, Ava still didn't see the sense in making the mistake of assuming he'd be okay with a visit at his home. In other words, she was going to pay it safe.

As the cab pulled away, Ava stood on the sidewalk for a moment. The house was located on an up-and-coming street. On the opposite side of the street, there were lots in mid-build. One house was actively being worked on as Ava stood there. The rain was still coming down, but it was little more than a mist—not nearly enough for an eager construction crew to call it a day. As she walked to the end of the street to stay out of view from anyone that might be peering out of the windows, it was one of the rare occasions where Ava wished she had a hat. Or at least an umbrella. She'd never really cared for either, thinking they were both a bit too dainty. And though she knew she had no trouble catching the eyes of men, she also never saw herself as the type that was pretty enough to *need* a hat in order to enhance what she was wearing. Besides, it wasn't like this police woman's uniform was flattering.

Just as she thought she may actually get drenched, the rain let up completely, leaving a faint earthy aroma and just a beat of mist in its wake. Ava had found her way to the end of the street where she perched by a large and rather awkward-looking construction truck. She'd seen many just like it in the city around some of the larger sites, where high-rise buildings seemed to be started on an almost daily basis.

She wasn't sure what she was waiting for. She was hoping to catch him coming out, or maybe even his wife. She figured any woman having married into the family would have a few things to say about the odd marital arrangement for Penny Pickett and the peculiar family dynamics surrounding it. Of course, she knew there was no way she could stay out here, twiddling her thumbs and waiting, while Frank was in the city probably getting quite a bit done. If no one came out of the house in the next half an hour or so, she'd just knock.

Make a note of this, she told herself, although she couldn't help but hear it spoken in Clarence's voice. *When it comes to planning, you're pretty good. But it's the details that hang you up and if you don't fix it, they are going to get you in trouble. What if you came all the way out here and Kelvin isn't even home?*

It was a good question, and one she didn't want to face just yet. Besides, even Frank had though it was a good idea and—

Her thoughts derailed when she saw the front door open. Kelvin Pickett stepped out onto the porch. There was a briefcase in one hand and an umbrella in the other. He was dressed in a long coat with what looked like a very basic suit underneath. After getting a good look at the sky and seeing there was no rain, he reached back inside and left the umbrella. He called out something into the house (presumably to his wife) and the started down the stairs.

Ava waited, watching as Kelvin came to the edge of his yard and started down the sidewalk. The sidewalk, like most of the rest of the neighborhood, seemed unfinished as well. There were sections that were not yet complete, causing Kelvin to step out onto the wet street for a moment and then rejoin the sidewalk.

Ava watched him reach the end of the street from her little hiding place by the construction truck. When he turned right, Ava quickly stepped out onto the street and followed. She walked quickly, but not fast enough to draw the attention of the construction workers, and certainly not Kelvin Pickett. She stayed on the side of the street opposite where Kelvin had walked and when she came to the end, she looked to the right and saw Kelvin's shape already halfway down the block. She stood motionless and waited to see what he would do next. When he came to the next intersection, he continued straight ahead. Ava remained in place, watching as his figure got smaller. When he was two full blocks away, she started walking again. It was a good thing Wyatt River was fairly small because the small number of people on the streets made it easy to keep track of him.

Because of this, she was also able to notice that Kelvin seemed rather nervous. He walked briskly though not actually *fast.* He also took quick glances all around him, as if he wanted to make sure he wasn't being seen. It was quite odd, and made Ava realize that her hunch to wait him out to see what she could learn without knocking on his door had been the right one.

He took a left up ahead and when he was out of sight, Ava picked up a bit of speed. She could tell that the neighborhoods were quickly diminishing. If Kelvin's house was located in the good part of town, it took just two and a half blocks for Wyatt River's streets to lose their property values. The houses were more box-like, more ramshackle, though still respectable homes. And to Ava, it seemed that the poorer the neighborhood became, the more on edge Kelvin seemed to be.

Something was definitely up. Young men from wealthy families typically didn't carry briefcases into poor neighborhoods. A little stirring of excitement sparked in Ava's stomach. She kept in check as best as she could as she continued to tail Kelvin Pickett into the poor part of town.

***

Frank had to hand it to Ava. She'd been spot on with her assumption that the Duvalls might be more cooperative if she wasn't around. Not only because she was a woman in a position of power, but because she'd been the one to arrest Mack yesterday. When the Duvalls' maid answered the door, Betty Duvall was standing right behind her. It was almost as if she'd been expecting another visit from the police—and that her husband had instructed her to be a second set of eyes on the front door today.

"And what in God's name brings you here?" Betty asked, basically pushing the maid out of the way as she stormed towards Frank, still standing in the front door.

"I'd think that would be obvious, Mrs. Duvall. The investigation into Penny's death."

"Come to arrest more members of my family again, have you?"

"Not at all, Mrs. Duvall. I was hoping that here, in your home and without the Picketts around, I could have a talk. I know it's uncomfortable and probably makes you mad, but the fact of the matter is that the two best sources of what could have happened are your family and the Picketts. Right now, that's all we have to go on. Now…would you happen to know where Mr. Duvall is?"

"He's out settling some legal matters from the nonsense that occurred yesterday. Trying to clean up the mess that your partner

71

made…a partner I see didn't come along today. I hope it's because she was fired because of the scene she caused yesterday."

"Honestly, I'm not sure what the consequences were." It was an easy lie to tell because Betty Pickett was already getting on his nerves.

"Well, it doesn't matter. Mack isn't even here, as I said. If you want to speak to him, he may still be down at—"

"I think I'd actually rather speak to James."

"No. Absolutely not."

Frank waited a moment before he responded. He looked around at the elegant home, the sort of home he would never be able to afford for himself. He supposed living like this just made you start believing you truly were better than everyone else and that even the police and their investigations were beneath you. To that end, Frank was pretty sure he knew how to get his way: by playing into that belief.

"Mrs. Duvall, I understand your hesitancy, I really do." He took a step forward and lowered his voice—not because there was anyone around, but because he knew it tended to make people feel that they were part of some big secret. "But my hope is that maybe Penny revealed something to Jason. Maybe something secret…something her parents never even knew about."

A muted sort of understanding came across Betty's face as she slowly nodded. "I've sometimes wondered that myself, I have to admit. But he won't tell any secrets. He's a loyal boy and…"

"Well, I think there's a better chance that he'll talk if you or Mr. Duvall aren't around. I know it hurts to hear, but let's face it: there are things about a young man that he's not going to tell his parents."

She placed her hand on her chest as if this were a sudden revelation and it had broken her heart. She thought about it for a moment and then sighed. "Fine. You can talk to him. But I would make it short. If Mack comes home and you're talking to James one-on-one, I don't know how he'll react."

Frank nodded, keeping to himself how he didn't give a damn how Mack Duvall would react. "Is James here?"

"He is. He's been up in his room most of the day. I know it doesn't seem like it, but this whole thing has upset him quite a bit. He's just trying to remain strong." She looked to the right, to a winding staircase that led to a second floor that overlooked the first floor via an elegant iron railing. "His room is upstairs, third on the left."

"Thank you," Frank said, putting on his best sincere voice. He walked up the stairs, again realizing just how out of place he felt in a house like this. He found James's room exactly where Betty had said. The door was closed, so Frank knocked.

"Yes?" came the young man's voice.

Frank opened the door and found James Duvall sitting at a writing desk. He was pushing a small journal to the edge of the desk as he turned around. The expression on his face made it clear that the last person he expected to find at his door was a detective; clearly, he remembered Frank from yesterday. He looked alarmed, maybe even a little angry.

"It's okay," Frank said. "Your mother gave me permission. And I promise I'll make it quick. I was just hoping to have a chat with you while the Picketts weren't around. I know it was sort of crazy in their house yesterday."

"Well, I don't know anything. So I don't know how you think I can help."

"Well, let's find out." Frank took only two steps inside, since he had not been formally invited in. "It's just you and me here right now, James. I need you to tell me how you really felt about the marriage being called off. I'm talking *before* the murder. During the argument the night before, how did you feel about that?"

"It felt strange at first," James said, without thinking too much about it. "It had been this one goal my family had been working towards and then all of a sudden, it might not happen. Penny is great and all, but I wasn't excited about staking my entire future on her."

"You said 'Penny is great and all.' Were the two of you romantically interested in one another at all, or was it all just part of the plans of your families?"

"No, we didn't care for one another in that way. We were friendly just to appease our parents, but there was no romantic interest."

"So you were relieved when it was called off?"

"Yes, I was quite glad. But…not that she was killed. She didn't deserve that, and I'm very sad that she's gone."

"Your mother seems to think you're taking it hard."

James shrugged and thought about his next statement before saying it. "Because our families were always together, I saw her a lot. Penny was the first friend I've ever had that died. It feels very strange."

"You said you didn't want to have to plan your future around her. Do you know what might have happened later on? Had you and Penny secretly talked about perhaps separating at some point in the future?"

He smiled sadly. "Penny mentioned it a few times, in a sort of rebellious way. But I wouldn't even joke about it. I knew there was lots of money involved in it and by just marrying one another, Penny and I would be set for life. I was okay with that for the most part."

Frank mulled it all over. With this sudden reveal, the so-called arranged marriage didn't seem so cut and dry after all. Not only had the father of the bride-to-be been on the fence about the entire set-up, but now it turned out that the would-be groom and the bride had not been fully on board.

In other words, it seemed like Ava had been right after all. And he did not want to be the one to tell her.

CHAPTER FIFTEEN

The poorer neighborhoods and streets of Wyatt River became little more than dusty tracks. What was odd was that the worse condition the town was in, the more people lined the streets. Ava supposed these were people rushing about for jobs and errands, the busy center of the town. There were men in suits as well as panhandlers all on the same street, a stark contrast to what she'd seen on Fifth Avenue these last few days.

Because of the thicker body of traffic in this area, Ava was able to get closer to Kelvin and still not be seen. It also created more of an obstacle for her, though—so much so that when Kelvin took a left several more streets further ahead, Ava lost him. She came to a dusty intersection and scanned the streets. It was clear that he was nowhere ahead of her, where the street descended a slight hill and came to an end at what looked to be a newly plowed field ready for new construction of some kind. He'd obviously taken the right or the left at the next intersection, but she hadn't seen where he'd gone.

Well, he's got to come back, right? Again, she heard this as Clarence's voice, almost as if he were coaching her along in his head.

She thought he *would* need to come back, but maybe not necessarily in this same direction. But she figured she'd play the odds and stay where she was. It was clear from the way he'd been walking that he was up to something. And she suddenly found herself very interested in what he might have been carrying in that briefcase. It certainly did seem like something strange to carry in this part of town.

To do her best to not look suspicious, Ava purchased a newspaper from a newsie on the corner. When she gave the kid a nickel tip, he looked as if he' just discovered a pot of gold. She sat on a worn and dirty bench, pretending to read the paper but really just looking over the top of it in the direction of where she'd lost track of Kelvin.

When he reappeared roughly five minutes later, she almost didn't recognize him. He had changed clothes and was still holding the briefcase. The clothes he now wore were much more common—not quite those of a laborer, but certainly not something his father would have approved of.

He walked straight ahead from the way he was coming, so when Ava stood up and tucked her newspaper under her arm, she had to take a right to follow him. Kelvin headed down a mostly deserted street that was filled with a slight stench of sewage and a smell that was almost like burning tobacco. He walked to the end of this block and simply waited. He stood by a street sign and for a moment, Ava wondered if he'd somehow gotten lost in his own town.

But then another figure appeared. It was a woman, coming from behind a building to the right, further down the street. As she approached him, Kelvin turned and faced her. He still seemed slightly nervous but not nearly as twitchy and paranoid as he'd seemed before he'd made his quick stop to change clothes. The woman closed the distance between them and greeted him with a kiss. It was not just a little nip on the cheek; they kissed passionately, but briefly. Her arms went around his waist with the sort of familiarity that suggested they'd been there many times before.

The pair spoke briefly and then Kelvin took her hand. The fact that he was in a relationship wasn't a surprise. Kelvin was young and relatively good-looking, a cake eater if Ava had ever seen one. But he'd changed clothes for her—and in a way that severely downgraded his usual wardrobe. Something didn't add up here...

She had to take a risk and get closer. She hurried her pace, passing by a scant few others walking along the street. Still holding her newspaper, she at least had a way to quickly appear as if she was just a usual chick, going about her day if it came to that. But as she closed the distance to fifteen feet, and then even to ten, it was clear that Kelvin Pickett's complete and total concentration was on this woman.

Ava was close enough to hear fragments of the conversation. He sounded distressed as he spoke with her, and Ava assumed he was maybe venting about the death of his sister. Yet as she heard more and more fragments, Ava started to understand that he wasn't talking about his sister, but about his future. She was not able to hear every single word, but she heard more than enough to form a new opinion.

"...think I was so upset that...father had his eye on her to take his role. But he never...in the first place. I don't want the damned company and...or be the sole heir. Does that make me a bad person? Does that make me...understand it?"

So he truly never had any desire to run or own his father's company, Ava thought. Based on everything he said, there was no reason he'd want his father's business or would have any sort of gain or advantage to his sister being out of the picture.

His lady friend responded with a soft, sympathetic voice. "If you think…of your…and a normal life."

"That's all I want." It was the loudest he's spoken since the two had met.

With this bit of information, Ava stopped walking and let them get farther ahead. After a few more steps, she decided to let them go—to leave them to their privacy. Yes, the mystery of why he'd changed clothes before he met with this woman was strange indeed. Perhaps he was trying to live two lives at once to make her and his family happy at the same time.

If that were the case, Ava wished him the best. In the meantime, she thought she had more than enough to go back to Frank. Kelvin Pickett just wanted to live a normal life with a girl that was in a totally different societal class. George Pickett might see that as a crime, but Ava Gold certainly did not.

With enough evidence to rule Kelvin out, Ava turned around and started back up the dusty street, wondering how hard it might be to find a cab in this part of town. And also wondering what piece of this case she wasn't yet able to see.

CHAPTER SIXTEEN

She lucked out on finding a cab. All it took was a young buck staring her up and down and a quick flash of her smile. He'd not only pointed her to where a cab would be, but also offered to pay for it. She declined and when she left Wyatt River, she left a rather disappointed young man behind.

She spent the drive back to the city thinking about the sort of measures a man like Kelvin Pickett would have to take in order to live the proper, polished life his father expected while also trying to prove to his dame that he wanted no part of that life—that he only wanted her and the trappings of normalcy that came with it. It also made her wonder if there might even be a small part of Kelvin that was sad about his sister's passing only because there would now be more pressure on him to take up the mantle Penny would have taken.

Rather than head back to the precinct, Ava opted to take the cab back to Fifth Avenue. She and Frank had parted ways on rather heated terms so they'd not made plans on where to meet up again, but she figured if he wasn't still there, she'd place a call to the station and leave a message for him.

It was nearing three in the afternoon when the cab dropped her off on the other side of the street from the Pickett residence. Just like back in Wyatt River, the city still contained a bit of a pleasant earthy aroma from the recent rainfall. She approached the front door and just as she reached out to knock, a sudden memory came back to her. She thought of the little smudge she'd found in Penny's room—the smudge that looked almost like oil. She wondered if Frank had asked around about that today.

She knocked on the door and, as seemed to be the routine, it was answered by Evelyn. There was a rather somber look on her face but she managed a smile for Ava. "Detective Gold, is that right?"

"That's right. Is my partner here, by any chance? Frank Wimbly?"

"He is. I believe he's in the parlor, speaking with one of the women that was hired to help design Penny's dress."

"And he's been here all day?"

"A few hours. Mr. Pickett arrived home to find him here and was quite upset but he's calmed down since then." She then cast a look at

Ava that seemed to say: *But to keep it quiet, maybe you should stay out of his sight.*

It took some reorienting, but Ava managed to recall which of the large rooms was the parlor. Walking that way, she could already hear Frank speaking. She followed his voice and paused at the parlor entrance just as Frank finished asking a question. The woman sitting on the seat on the other side of the room was older, maybe in her late fifties, and dressed as if she were going overseas to meet the Queen. The dress she was wearing probably cost more than Ava would make in a year.

"…before or after you arrived?" Frank was asking.

"No, sir," the well-dressed woman said. "I spoke with Mrs. Pickett shortly before I left, but that was all."

"And there were no cross words?"

"No, sir. If anything, it was quite positive. She was very happy with the dress I'd brought her."

Frank finally turned slightly to his right and saw Ava. He then turned back to the other woman and nodded politely. "Thank you for your time. This has been very helpful."

When the woman got up, she looked very happy to be done with this task. Passing by Ava, the woman barely even glanced her way. Ava walked into the parlor and sat where the other woman had been sitting. Without the frills and lace of the woman's dress, the chair looked much larger.

"The dress maker?" Ava asked.

"Yeah, that was her. I also spoke with the baker the Pickett's hired and the interior decorator—everyone that had been in and out of the house yesterday morning before it was discovered that Penny had been murdered. And I got nothing of use. The only thing worth mentioning is that the interior designer was quite upset when George suggested he'll not be paying for their planning, seeing as how there won't be a party." He reclined back a bit more on the little sofa he was perched on and sighed. "You? Anything worth mentioning out in Wyatt River?"

"Yes," she said. But before she could go on, she knew she had to do something. Seeing Frank so disappointed to have no breaks or leads after half a day of conversations made her realize that he was just as invested in this as she was. And this morning, she'd lost her temper at him because of her own hang-ups: the way being in this part of New York City made her feel, as well as the drama back at home with the threats from the mob and her failure to find anything new about the man that had likely killed Clarence. She'd taken it out on Frank, and only because he'd been trying to watch out for her.

"You okay there, Gold?"

She didn't realize she was taking so long to form the right words. She'd never been very good at apologizing. "I think I need to apologize for this morning. If we're going to be successful on this case, we need to communicate well. This morning, I let personal matters cloud my mood and I lashed out at you. I hate to admit it, but…I was wrong to do it."

Frank waved the comment off with his hand, as if he were swatting away a bug. "Not a big deal at all." He took off his derby hat, wiped his brow with a handkerchief he pulled from his pocket, and placed the hat back on his head. He did not appear to be sweating, which made Ava assume it was some sort of nervous habit he'd picked up over the years. "I can't imagine the stress you must be under. I mean, to be fair, you asked for it. But, still…you're my partner and I did it to support you as such. I just ask that you do the same for me from here on out."

"Of course," she said. There was a fleeting moment where she nearly felt the words coming to her tongue—to tell him about what was going on with the mob and how she had visited a woman in the hospital that may have very well been attacked by the same man that had killed Clarence. But she held it all back. That was a topic for another time. They were here to find Penny Pickett's killer, not rummage through her personal demons.

"So…Wyatt River?"

"I was able to follow Kelvin when he left his home and found out a bit of news." She told him about how she followed Kelvin Pickett into the poorer part of the town and how he'd made a quick stop somewhere along the way to change clothes. When she got to the part about meeting with the woman and the bits of conversation she'd picked up, a look of disappointment crossed Frank's face.

"Why the frown?" she asked. "Isn't it a good thing to prove someone is innocent?"

"The easy answer is 'yes.' But not when you're quickly eliminating every single potential suspect on a very short list."

"Have you been to Penny's room today?" Ava asked.

"Just a quick peek in. Nothing extensive."

"I think I'd like to have another look. If we're not having any luck with finding anything from *people*, maybe there's something else. Like that streak of grease, for instance."

"Might as well go on up, then. And if we can do it and get out without having to speak to George, even better. I've just about had my fill of that man for one day."

They walked up together, Ava noticing right away that Frank was allowing her to take the lead. Going up the stairs seemed different today. Without the wailing of Millie Pickett or the tension of knowing George was watching her every move, it almost felt like they were actually wanted and being of some use.

She found the room the same as it was the day before. Already, it had the feel of a place of loss, a place that would hold great reverence once day. Nothing had been touched, nothing had been moved. Ava walked over to the far wall, standing in the corner. She looked down to where she'd seen the odd smudge the day before and could not find it. Thinking perhaps it was harder to see now that the sun was coming through the window at a different angle, Ava tried a few different positions but still did not see it. Getting on her hands and knees and running her finger across the area she'd seen it revealed the same thing: the smudge was gone.

"It's been cleaned up," Ava said, looking up to Frank.

"Are you serious?"

"It's gone." She got to her feet and looked around the room, puzzled. "I know I didn't give specific instructions not to alter anything in the room yesterday. Did you?"

"No. But it would be common sense, right? Good Lord…do you think it was cleaned up intentionally?"

Ava shrugged, still looking at the spot on the floor. "It didn't seem like a big deal yesterday. I just thought it was maybe some sort of makeup or maybe even polish of some kind."

"Shoe polish, maybe?" Frank asked.

Ava instantly looked to the closet on the right side of the room. She walked over to it and opened the door. Several dresses hung inside, along with a few braziers and gowns. Sitting on the floor beneath it all were six pairs of shoes. Two pair were very fancy slippers with heels— not the sort of shoe that would receive any sort of traditional polish. The others consisted of two pairs of Mary Janes and a set of traditional flappers. Their condition made it quite clear that while Penny had taken good care of her shoes, none of them had been polished recently. Ava even reached in to take them out, smelling them and confirming that they did not smell like shoe polish. She turned to Frank and shook her head.

"Well, we know George or Millie sure as hell didn't do any cleaning," Frank said.

Curious, Ava walked back over to the window. There were a few slight smudges around the frame and one single, small streak along the bottom. "The window hasn't been cleaned," she said.

Frank grinned for just a moment and then composed himself. Ava thought it might be a sign that he'd been impressed she'd even thought to look for such a thing. "So the floor was cleaned, but the window wasn't. And if you're a maid, wouldn't you clean the entire room all at once?"

"I'm not sure," Ava said. "Maybe we should find out. Did you speak with Evelyn today?"

"Yes. For about half an hour, trying to learn about the comings and goings around the house. I even grilled her hard about where she was on the night the murder occurred. She gave enough information where it'll be very easy to check her alibis. And in the time I was here today, I never once saw her go upstairs."

"But I'm going to assume any work she'd done in the past day or so never came up, right?"

"Right, but I did find that Evelyn isn't the only hired help in the Pickett household. There's also a hired chef and a valet. There had also been a second maid up until three weeks ago, when the second one quit because of her advanced age."

"You get names for all of them?" Ava asked.

"Sure did. I might even know where to find a few of them." He checked his watch and this time when he grinned at her, he let it stay on his face. "The evening is winding down, though. You think we should split up again?"

CHAPTER SEVENTEEN

It was easy enough to locate George Pickett's valet. As sad as it seemed, he was at the tailor's shop, making sure George's suit for Penny's funeral would be properly adjusted before his daughter was put into the ground. The valet's name was Raymond Dove, a thirty-eight year-old man that looked closer to fifty. When Ava found him at the tailor's shop, he seemed high strung and very nervous.

She was able to identify him easily enough, by simply flashing her badge at the woman behind the counter. The reaction she got form the woman was a drastic change from what she'd been getting from the men of this city. The woman seemed almost *proud* of her and was more than happy to point out Mr. Pickett's valet.

Raymond Dove was sitting on a chair along the far right wall, nervously tapping his foot on the wooden floor while he read the day's paper. His hair was dapper and well maintained, just like the button-down shirt and black pants he wore. When Ava approached him, he looked up at her with the sort of rapt attention a man always looking over his shoulder might display.

"Are you Mr. Raymond Dove?" Ava asked.

"I am. And who's asking?" he looked irritated that he'd been bothered but also slightly concerned.

She subtly showed her him her badge, not wanting to make a big production out of it. Raymond looked at it as if Ava had performed an amazing magic trick. "I'm Detective Ava Gold. I was hoping to ask you some questions about Penny Pickett and what happened to her."

The statement clearly shocked him and it was the last thing he'd expected to hear. "I'm sure you can understand that we have been instructed not to discuss this matter with anyone outside of the family."

"Even the police?" Ava pressed.

Raymond had nothing to say to that. He looked past Ava, back to the main counter as if willing George's suit to be ready. Ava decided to continue, to keep talking as if Raymond had invited her to do so. So far, he was not striking her as the type to cause a scene or put up much of a fight.

"How long have you been working as Mr. Pickett's valet?"

He looked nervously at her but he seemed to be one of the few men in town that respected a badge regardless of the gender of the person that was carrying it. "Going on two years now."

"Is he a good man to work for? A fair man?"

"Absolutely. Working for him has changed my life for the better."

"Have you ever seen him lose his temper?"

"A few times. Mostly with things related to work. The man is very passionate about his business."

Ava didn't like these answers. It felt far too much like speaking to an actor that was reading off of a very specific script. She figured it was time to try to trip him up. "Were you inside the house at all on the morning Penny's body was found?"

"No. I wasn't due to arrive at their home at all that day, not until Mr. Pickett was finished with work for the day. I did have a few tasks to run around town, though."

"Were those tasks associated with Penny's coming out party?"

"Yes. Nearly all of them, in fact."

"Do you recall the last time you saw Penny?"

Raymond thought about this for a moment. The rapid-fire innocent questions seemed to be putting him at ease. "Day before yesterday. I was bringing in Mr. Pickett's new supply of shaving creams. Penny was having tea with Bill Laskey in the kitchen. They invited me for a cup, but I passed."

"Who is Bill Laskey?"

"The main cook. He and Penny got along famously. I suppose you could say just about everyone that works for the Picketts got along well with her. She was a sweet girl. Always good for a joke or a laugh, always wanting to see how she could help others. Damn shame what happened to her."

"Mr. Dove, one more question, if you don't mind. On the morning it was discovered Penny had been killed, where were you?"

"I was at the factory, getting some of Mr. Pickett's financial statements ready for a meeting with the bank later that day. It wasn't until I got to the bank that I heard the news."

"How many people do you think you interacted with between the factory and the bank?"

This question seemed to clue Raymond in to the exact information Ava was trying to find. He looked hurt and the tone of his voice changed drastically. "Maybe three or four. I was at the factory from about six thirty or so until eight. I then took a cab to the bank where I was scheduled to meet Mr. Pickett. I was there, speaking with an account manager, for about half an hour before I received the news about Penny."

"Thank you, Mr. Dove. Now, I understand there is a maid that quit working for the Picketts a few weeks back. Do you recall her name?"

This, too, was something of a trick. Ava knew the woman's name because Frank had given it to her just before they'd gone their separate ways. She just wanted to see how truthful and helpful Raymond Dove truly was.

"Esther Roberts," he said, giving the name freely—likely just to get the detective off of his case.

"By any chance do you happen to know where she lives?"

"I do, actually. I don't know the actual address, but she's out on Statesman Avenue in that ugly brown building by the butcher's shop."

"Thank you very much," she said, turning and heading for the door. She knew exactly the area Raymond was talking about, as her father's gym was just two blocks off of Statesman Avenue and often got meat from that very same butcher.

She headed back out onto the street and decided against the cab. The walk would take about fifteen or twenty minutes, but that was fine. She recalled the first two days on the job, when she'd still been in the WB. Back then, she and Frances had walked several miles in the course of a day and now, just a few short weeks later, she found that she almost enjoyed walking around all of these different streets that were becoming familiar to her.

Still, it was summer and though the earlier drizzle of rain had cooled things down a bit, she was sweating slightly when she reached Statesman Avenue. She came to the building Raymond Dove had mentioned and stepped inside. The place was set up like an apartment building but wasn't *quite* an apartment building. The first floor contained three rooms right off of the small, cramped lobby. A flight of stairs led to the second and, based on the height of the exterior, she assumed a third floor waited above that.

However, Frank had mentioned the woman having to step down from working with the Picketts because of her advanced age. To Ava, it just made sense that an older woman would live on the main floor so walking up and down the stairs would not be part of her everyday routine. Taking a chance, Ava went to the first door and knocked. She figured she'd check every apartment in the place if she had to but she hoped a helpful neighbor could point her in the right direction if it came to that.

The first door she knocked on offered no results. She knocked a second time and still, no one came to the door. She then tried the second door. She knocked and got an answer right away. An elderly voice called through the door, sounding both pleasant and ragged all at once.

"Hey there! Coming, coming..." There was the slight sound of shuffling from inside and then the same voice came again, closer this time. "Yeah, who's out there?"

"My name is Ava Gold. I'm a detective with the New York Police Department."

The laugh that followed this from the other side of the door did not offend Ava at all. It was good-natured and filled with joy—if not also just a bit of disbelief. "Well, you sound like a woman!"

"I *am* a woman, ma'am!"

"Uh huh. You trying to get one over on me, child?"

"Not at all. I can show you my badge if you like."

With the laugh tapering off, the woman on the other side opened the door. It only opened about a foot or so, allowing a small-statured African American lady to peek out. Her eyes showed signs of aging, but also of curiosity. "They hiring dames now, are they?"

"A few."

The woman—Esther Roberts, according to Raymond Dove—cackled at this and stomped her foot in amusement. She opened the door, revealing more of her face and her hunched posture. The poor woman walked with a hump in her back and shoulders so scrunched up that they seemed to be almost up to her ears.

"Come on in, lady. You said Gold, right?"

"Yes ma'am."

She entered the apartment and instantly smelled cornbread and strong coffee. The front door entered through the kitchen and from what Ava could tell, the apartment consisted of only the kitchen, a small, adjoined living space that included what served as the bedroom, and a small bathroom off to the back. Esther pointed to one of two chairs sitting at a very small table, just inside the kitchen.

"Go on and have a sit," she said.

Ava did, finding that the smell of the cornbread was making her hungry. She ignored it and started her questioning right away. "So sorry to bother you, ma'am, but are you Esther Roberts?"

"Sure am. Did I break the law and didn't even know about it?" She settled herself carefully down in the other chair, where an already-in-progress cup of coffee was waiting.

"Not at all. I don't know if you've heard or not, but Penny Pickett was murdered. I'm looking into that case."

"I did hear. Just last night, in fact. Damn shame. She was a fine little girl. Maybe tied a little too tight, but just as kind as you can imagine. She treated me more like an actual human than most of those other rich folks, that's for sure."

"How long did you work for the Picketts?"

"Almost six years. I should have quit sooner than I did, but that money is hard to come by these days, you know."

"I heard you quit because of your age, is that right?"

"Mostly. But it was in part because I just didn't like dealing with George and all of his rich friends. Always talking about their cases and running their jaw about how they could own the whole city if they wanted." She chuckled here and slapped the table, sloshing out a bit of her coffee. "George! Ain't that something? Been calling that joker *Mr. Pickett, sir* for so damn long, it feels awful good to call him by his name. *George!* Ha!"

"Would it surprise you to know that neither family—the Picketts or the Duvalls—seem to appreciate the fact that the police were trying to ask questions to find their killer."

"Hell no! You look pretty, sweetie, but that's an ignorant question. Too many questions and coppers around means someone might get a peek into their personal lives."

"What would they try to hide?"

"Oh, you name it! *George* pays his employees absolute garbage for the most part. Oh, and he's a pretty frequent customer to a few of the can houses around here, you know?"

"Can house?" Ava asked. She was pretty sure she'd heard the term before but the meaning of it was lost on her now. It was street slang for something…but she wasn't sure what.

"Bordellos, little girl. Whorehouses. And listen…I don't know for sure, but I think there might have been some spouse-swapping going on between them two families. They're close and friendly for sure, but I think there's a reason they're so tight. Each one is afraid the other will spill all the dirt at the first sign of trouble or argument."

"What can you tell me about the relationship between Mr. Pickett and Penny?"

The humor and grit went out of her as she sipped from her coffee and absorbed the question. "That's the one thing I'll never give the man grief over. He loved his kids something fierce…especially Penny.

Treated her like a queen. It was more than spoiling her rotten, though. He was a good father, as simple as that."

Ava was almost hoping Esther would report this. It lined right up with the story of how George had come right to his daughter's side when she'd mentioned wanting to call off the arranged marriage.

"And what about the Duvalls? Did you ever see any interactions between them and Penny?"

"Well, o'course you know Penny and James were arranged to be married, right? That's another of those things the families were trying to keep secret."

"Yes ma'am, I knew that."

"Then there's Betty Duvall, who has all the personality of a flat rock, and Mack. Now, if you're trying to figure out if it was either of those two that killed Penny, I can close that case for you now. Mack Duvall has no guts at all. He won't even go deer hunting with his rich pals upstate because he hates the idea of the blood and all that. He's a bit of a sissy-boy. No way in hell is he *ever* going to kill someone. I doubt the man has ever even been in a fight."

"Is there anyone that ever came in and out of their home that you think *might* have it in them? Maybe someone that Mr. Pickett didn't get along with?"

"I tried thinking of that very same thing when I heard Penny had been killed and I hate to tell you, but I came up with nothing. The Picketts were very particular about who they invited into their home. Outside of the Duvalls and a few banker-types, that was about it."

Ava let all of this sink in, trying to figure out if there were any further questions Esther could answer. The fact that the Picketts seemed to keep their circle of friends and trusted associates small was making this much harder than it had to be.

"You look troubled," Esther said. "I suppose a case can't be easy when you have people like the Duvalls and Picketts at the center of all the questioning, right?"

"Pretty much," Ava said. She got to her feet and started for the door, looking back to the kind lady at the table. "Thank you for your help, ma'am."

"No problem at all. And thank *you*. I know it can't be easy being a copper in this city *and* a woman on top of that. If you'll take it, I'd like to send you off with some cornbread. Just came out of the oven."

It was, so far, the brightest part of Ava's day. "You know, that would be fantastic."

Esther set about cutting out a piece from her cast-iron skillet while Ava's mind started to swirl, trying to think of what she and Frank could have possibly missed.

CHAPTER EIGHTEEN

At roughly the same time Ava was knocking on the door of Mrs. Esther Roberts, Frank was sitting down once again in the parlor of the Pickett home. He hated that this place was starting to feel like his office. But at the same time, he'd noticed that George Pickett seemed to keep himself away when Ava wasn't around. He'd been relieved when George had stayed in his office for the fifteen minutes or so Ava *had* come by.

So now here he was, sitting down across from a man that looked to be somewhere just north of fifty years old. His name was Rufus Carlin and he currently worked as a butler and secondary assistant to George Pickett. Frank had not even been aware of the man's existence until he came by earlier in the day to deliver a certain wine that George ordered special from overseas. Sitting on the other side of the parlor from Frank, Rufus Carlin did not seem nervous but he *did* look out of his element. He had the sort of eyes that made him look as if he might sneeze at any moment, squinted close to shut, but not quite. He had the beginnings of a beard that were so slight that it made Frank wonder if the man had simply forgotten to shave a few days ago. Rufus looked around as if waiting for someone to pop up and tell him that this was all an elaborate joke.

"With your job duties," Frank said, "how often are you here at the house? Based on my own presence here over the last few days, I assume you're not here all day on a daily basis. Is that correct?"

"That's right. Some weeks I'm not even here at all. I usually only come to the house when Raymond has a busy week or during times when Mr. Pickett has to be out of town."

"So you were not here on the day or night Penny was killed?"

"That's right. In fact, when I came in to deliver the wine earlier today, that was the first time I'd been here in four or five days."

"And would Mr. and Mrs. Pickett back that up?" Asking this question, Frank realized that there was something about the butler that was chewing at him. Not his appearance, and nothing he'd said so far, but something else.

"Absolutely," Rufus said, nodding emphatically.

"And how well do you know the Duvalls? Do you have any interactions with them?"

"I see them from time to time, but not enough to really know them that well. I get the feeling that Mr. Duvall doesn't care for me."

"Any reason why?"

Rufus frowned and shook his head. "I'd assume because he's rich and tends to look down on just about anyone."

"With your odd schedule, do you ever happen to see other people coming in and out of the house? Maybe other delivery men or people from Mr. Pickett's factory?"

Rufus thought about this for a good amount of time—long enough so that Frank believed the man when he finally answered. "I can't say that I have. I did run into one of the seamstresses that had been hired to work on Penny's dress the last time I was here, but that's it. Honestly, it's pretty much just the Duvalls."

Frank nodded, sensing this particular line of questioning had come to an end. As he was about to get to his feet, he finally realized what it was about Rufus Carlin that had been sitting oddly with him. It was his name. The last name, in particular.

"Mr. Carlin, tell me…for some reason, your name sticks out to me. *Carlin.* Is there any reason I might have heard it somewhere before?"

Rufus seemed surprised and a little entertained by this. "Not that I can think of."

"Do you get that reaction a lot?"

"Can't say that I do." He seemed to be thinking about it a bit himself but then shrugged. "I'm really no one of any importance…as my job proves."

Frank wasn't sure why the name stuck with him so strong, but Rufus did seem genuinely confused by the question. "Mr. Carlin, thank you so much for your time. I do appreciate it."

"Of course. I certainly hope you're able to find who did this. From what I knew of Penny, she was a very bright and special young lady."

Rufus excused himself and left the room. Frank followed instantly after, done with this house for the time being. He was sure he and Ava would end up in it again before the case was solved, but he was happy to be done with it for the day. He considered walking to the study to let George Pickett know he was leaving, but decided against it. He simply left the message with Evelyn, who he found sweeping the stairs, and headed out.

The day had gotten late, the heat cooling a bit and the sky looking as if it might consider a bit more rain later in the afternoon. Frank drove the precinct car back to the station, running the name of Rufus Carlin over and over in his head. What was it about that last name that was pricking his brain so?

He parked the car in the lot, noticing that a few of the other cars had also been taken out. He wondered when all police might have cars at their disposal. The city was growing so fast, and more and more money was being thrown at the NYPD in an effort to keep up with the growing population. Certainly a car for every cop would be a necessity before long.

As he walked around to the front of the building, he saw that he and Ava's timing seemed to be spot on. She was coming around the corner, coming from the west, just as he started up the stairs. He could tell by the look on her face that she'd had just as much luck as he'd had. He waited for her and she hurried her pace to meet him.

"Any luck?" she asked.

"No. You?"

"None."

As they started walking up the stairs together, Frank figured he'd take a shot. If the name *Carlin* was bothering him, maybe it would ring a few bells with someone else as well. "Hey, Gold, does the name Rufus Carlin mean anything to you?"

She thought about it for a moment as he held the precinct door open for her. "No, I don't think so."

"What about just the last name?"

"Carlin?" She chewed on it as they passed by the front desk and made their way into the bullpen area. "I don't think so. Why?"

"I interviewed the butler and secondary assistant to Pickett just now. Rufus Carlin. The last name is about to make me go goofy. It seems familiar for some reason."

They walked to his desk together and Frank noticed that Ava was getting fewer stares these days. He guessed it meant the other bulls were getting used to her. He sank down into his chair and continued to chew on the name. *Carlin...Carlin.* When an older cop walked by, a gentleman about a year away from retirement named Gault, Frank took another shot.

"Hey, Gault. Does the name Carlin mean anything to you? As a last name, that is?"

Gault considered it for a moment, his pudgy cheeks looking like the jowls of a bulldog. "Nah, I don't think so. The only Carlin I know is Carlin Whiskey." He chuckled and shook his head. "But that's long gone now, I guess. Fuckin' prohibition."

Frank clicked his fingers and sat straight up. "Hot damn, that's it! Thanks, Gault."

Gault smiled and walked away. "Glad to help," he said over his shoulder.

"Want to fill me in?" Ava asked.

"That's why the name stuck out to me. Carlin Whiskey. It was a really popular brand of whiskey before prohibition came along."

"Does it mean anything?"

"I think it just might," Frank said, getting up and walking quickly towards the records. "And we can start with the fact that Rufus Carlin played dumb. He acted like he was a nobody."

"Well, if the company went out of business because of prohibition, maybe he is."

"Yeah, but usually someone from a family like that—a popular family with even the slightest bit of fame attached to it—doesn't tend to *not* talk about it. right?"

"Maybe. But isn't there a chance he's from a different Carlin family?"

"Maybe. And I bet it will only take us a few minutes to find out."

In tandem, they got up and headed for the records room. It was not a part of the station that Ava was very familiar with, having only been inside once, so she was quite excited to use it properly.

The records room sat to the far-left side of the station, occupying a small room. The room's walls were mostly covered up by bemouth-looking filing cabinets that Ava had to wrestle with to get some of the drawers to open. A large, battered desk sat in the middle of the room for officers to go through whatever records they were studying.

It did not take long for them to discover that there weren't many records to help them with a search for the Carlin family, but Ava was surprised to find that there were enough forms and registrations for the business to give an overview of the story. Not only was Carlin Whiskey a hot name before prohibition, but the Carlin family had been among the elite Fifth Avenue families. They'd found the information easily enough, flipping through folders and steel drawers of bulky black, steel cabinets that lined three of the room's four walls.

"That might be another reason the last name was sticking out in my head…or trying to, anyway," Frank said. "They were right there in the midst of the Picketts, right on Fifth Avenue."

"Why are there prints of all of these registrations?" Ava asked.

"Because of prohibition. Anyone making liquor was required to register and then give proof that they were no longer creating it. The—"

There was a knock on the door and they both turned to find Captain Minard standing there. "I saw you two rushing in here. Please tell me there's some kind of a lead on the Pickett case."

"I came across a guy named Rufus Carlin today," Frank said. "The name stuck out to me and I wasn't sure why. I'm looking into Carlin Whiskey. They were a big Fifth Avenue family, right?"

"Oh yeah," Minard said, stepping inside the room. "And that family took a huge hit after prohibition. The Carlins went broke pretty quickly after that. Thomas Carlin, the owner of the company, tried getting lucky with some sort of gambling and then started selling his whiskey illegally. He killed himself when the cops came calling."

"That's right," Frank said, excitedly, as if it was all coming back to him. "I had just started the force back then…1921. Jesus, no wonder the name was so familiar. Chief…do you happen to know if there was anyone in the family named Rufus?"

"You know, I don't know for sure. Check the registrations and see if he's on there anywhere."

Ava held up the copy she'd started reading over when Minard had come in. "We're already on it."

Now just as curious and caught up in the excitement as his detectives, Minard came into the room. He had barely come over long enough to cast a shadow over Ava before she saw the name right there at the bottom of the sheet. It was hard to read because it had been signed, but it was unmistakable.

"He's right here," she said. "His signature is right here, under Thomas Carlin."

"Are there any other names?" Minard asked, politely taking the form from her. He looked it over, already shaking his head. "No. No other names. It seems Rufus Carlin was Thomas Carlin's son."

"So that means he would have been the heir had Thomas died and prohibition had never come along?"

"Seems that way," Minard said, handing him the form. "Why?"

With a beam of excitement in his eye, Frank grinned and said: "Because less than an hour ago, he was telling me he wasn't anybody important."

He and Ava started for the door right away, leaving the records out on the little table in the center of the room.

"Tread carefully, would you?" Minard said. "The last thing I need is for those rich assholes calling me with more complaints." He then cut his eyes specifically at Ava and added, "Especially if they have legitimate points about hasty accusations and arrests."

"Yes, sir," Ava said as they made their way out of the room.

They rushed out of the building and back out onto the street. Ava had nearly forgotten about their access to one of the precinct cars and started walking briskly in the direction of Fifth Avenue—which would be one hell of a hike at this time of the day as people started filling the streets on their way home from work.

It was a bit maddening to sit in the passenger's seat while Frank did his best to make his way through traffic; pedestrians, a few horse-drawn carts, and other cars were all in the way and Frank did an impressive job of getting around it all.

"You think the Picketts will be happy to see us again?" Ava asked.

"Oh, at this point I really don't care," Frank said. "I do think we need to heed Captain Minard's advice, though. I think we need to *really* be careful how we act and what we say when we get there."

Ava felt the need to argue this, but kept her mouth shut. She simply had to accept that people with lots of money were indeed somewhat above the law. It was unfortunate, but Ava felt she'd done a decent job of getting adjusted to men looking down on her even with her job as a detective, so she was used to being seen as second-class.

Not yet accustomed to the convenience of an automobile, Ava found herself astounded at just how fast they were able to cover the distance between the precinct and Fifth Avenue. It had taken about fifteen minutes and Frank had only one near-accident when he'd come less than six inches away from running into a newsboy that was rushing across the street. When they arrived at the Pickett residence, Frank did seem to have a bit of difficulty with parking but managed to get it right after three attempts. They hurried out of the car and Frank was knocking on the door the moment Ava joined him on the doorstep.

When the door opened, Evelyn was there to greet them. She had a tired expression on her face; Ava could only imagine the amount of shouting and crying the poor woman had endured over the last two days, on top of everything George and Millie Pickett demanded of her. Worry instantly crowded into her eyes. She did not verbally say it, but the look in her eyes seemed to say: *"Really? You two again? Are you intentionally trying to piss this family off?"*

"Good afternoon, Evelyn," Frank said. "By any chance, is Mr. Carlin still here?"

"He is, sir. I believe he's in the parlor. Come on in."

She ushered them in quickly, perhaps hoping they could get in, do what needed to be done, and then get out without George or Millie seeing them. As it turned out, though, there was no chance at all of this happening. As soon as Ava stepped in behind Frank, she saw George Pickett standing just outside of the foyer, looking into the parlor. When he heard the door closing behind Ava and then the footsteps of the two detectives, he turned to face them. Irritation settled on his face at once. Shaking his head, he started walking their way.

"No. Absolutely not. I've given you full access to this house in the midst of our loss and it's getting out of hand."

"I understand that," Frank said. He then took a step closer to George and lowered his voice a bit. "But we have a potential lead now. Something has come up in the past several minutes."

George's irritation flickered and he cast his eyes to Ava, then back to Frank. "What sort of lead?"

"I can't give you the exact details until we know for sure. But for right now, we need to speak with Mr. Carlin."

"You mean Rufus? No. I don't know what you think he's done, but I can assure you, he—"

"Sir, it's quite alright," Rufus interrupted him, stepping into the foyer. He looked to Frank, trying to look confused and perplexed. But even Ava could see that he was trying a little too hard to look that way. He was acting…and not doing a very good job of it.

George looked confused as well, as he was *not* acting. Behind the anger and irritation, Ava could see that he was tired. And, of course, he was profoundly sad at the loss of his daughter and still wrestling with how to behave and present himself.

"Do what you want, then," he sneered at all three of them. "But not here. Not in my house. Take it outside. I'm…I'm done with this."

As if to put an exclamation point on this, he waved both hands at the trio like an aggravated child and stormed away in the direction of his office. Meanwhile, Evelyn looked at them apologetically and opened the front door for them. Ava led the way out and she noted that Frank made sure to stay behind Rufus, making sure he didn't try to make a quick escape.

Not wanting to test George Pickett's limits, Ava stepped down onto the street, opting not to speak with Rufus on the steps. Frank and Rufus followed suit, and Frank started in on the man right away.

"When I spoke to you not an hour and a half ago, you told me that you had no idea why your last name might sound familiar to me," Frank said, doing his best to remain calm. "You told me that you were no one important."

"That's right, sir," he said. He still did his best to seem confused but the acting job remained poor.

"Your father was Thomas Carlin," Ava said. "You would have been the heir to Carlin Whiskey if the company had not gone bankrupt and folded."

"That is also right."

"So why were you trying to mislead me?" Frank asked. "My partner and I are in the middle of a pressing murder investigation. A little truth would be helpful."

"Why would my family's failed business be of any consequence in this case?" Rufus said. "If you know any of the history behind it, especially the details about the demise of my father, I imagine you can see why I don't like talking about it."

"Yes, but you once lived here, on Fifth Avenue and these stretches of wealthy streets," Frank said. "Your connection to that and the social circles of the area tie you a bit closer to the Picketts as far as I'm concerned."

Ava had a thought and she did not think it through before saying it. It was simply a point that came to her and she felt it was quite important. "Being that you are from a well-to-do family and are now working for the Picketts makes me wonder if there was any connection between your families."

Saying this, Ava's eyes travelled to the lamppost where she'd watched as immigrant being chastised by three wealthy men. It was hard to imagine Rufus Carlin among that sort but then again, she also knew how money could corrupt people. She needed to look no further than the Picketts and Duvalls to see evidence of that.

"Is that the case?" Frank asked.

Rufus looked slightly embarrassed now. He seemed to be struggling with an answer, perhaps even finding one and then deciding not to speak it.

"I'll level with you," Frank said. "Your blatant lies from earlier make you a possible suspect for the murder of Penny Pickett. There's no hard evidence, but at this point your dishonesty is enough. So if you want to avoid that, I suggest you start talking right now."

Panic flooded Rufus's face instantly. "Yes, I was set to take the distillery over when dad stepped down—something he planned to do at the age of sixty. But, of course, prohibition came along and changed all of that. Dad killed himself when he was just fifty-four and by then, Carlin Whiskey was pretty much just as dead as he was. It took about five months for our family to lose everything. It all came apart so fast and we…we didn't know what to do. Mom had a heart attack shortly after and I found myself suddenly homeless. I knew I needed a job, so I worked down at the docks for a while and hated it. I'd never been used to manual labor because of our wealth and…well, this job with the Picketts came along and I took it. My dad and George knew one another rather well and I think they did it out of respect. And, God…I wanted the job because I missed the lifestyle. Just to be around it…that was enough."

Ava kept the comment to herself, but this sounded pathetic to her. This man would rather be a servant to the rich than to not be around these snobby social circles at all.

"What sort of interactions have you had with Penny while you've been working here?" Frank asked.

"Barely any. She stays to herself, mostly. And, as I said, I'm really not here at the house very often."

Ava believed it. And even if he *had* been at the house quite a bit, she still doubted Rufus Carlin would have killed Penny. He was so desperate to be around this scene that he'd never do anything to jeopardize it.

The tone of Frank's voice made Ava think he was putting these same pieces together. There was resistance in it—the sound of another lead slowly slipping away from them. "Can you provide your whereabouts on the night Penny was murdered?"

"Yes. From about ten to one in the morning, I was playing a bit of poker. After that, I went back home to my apartment."

"Can you give the names of people you played poker with?" Frank asked.

"And anyone that can verify you were indeed at your apartment for the remainder of the night?"

"Aye, I sort of had a little tumble in the bedroom with a broad from my old distillery days. I can give you her name, but I'd appreciate some privacy on it. She's engaged, you see…"

Ava nodded, looking to the ground, *God, are all men this hopeless?* It made her miss Clarence, who suddenly seemed to be far superior to just about any man she'd met since joining the force.

Rufus Carlin gave the names of five men he played poker with, as well as the engaged woman. As he wrote them down, Ava figured they'd end up contacting them all, but it would just be a formality. She was certain standing there in front of the Pickett home that Rufus Carlin was certainly not their man…which meant they were back at the start. No leads, no hope, and no answers.

CHAPTER NINETEEN

That night, Ava and Jeffrey stayed at her father's apartment once again. Jeffrey took it a bit easier this time, as it had now started to become almost like an adventure to him. Roosevelt seemed happy to have them there, too, though he was constantly apologetic about the state of the place. Ava was so tired when she finally allowed herself to sit down on the couch that she didn't even notice the state of the apartment or most of her father's apologies and excuses.

In fact, the majority of the night was a tired blur to her. The one thing she was able to truly focus on was the reason that she and Jeffrey were here at all. Caught up in the rapid whirlwind of disappointment that was the Penny Pickett case, she'd nearly forgotten about the large, dead rat the mob had placed at her front door. Toss in anonymous threats from fellow cops as well as reports and whispers of the man that may have killed her husband, and it almost made sense she'd slink back to her father's apartment for refuge.

She fell asleep sitting up on the couch and when she woke up, it was slightly after four in the morning. her back ached from the position she'd taken up on the couch and her heart stung with the guilt of knowing she'd not helped get Jeffrey to bed. She saw that her father was conked out in his throne, snoring lightly. At some point during the night, he'd placed a blanket over her.

She tiptoed into his very small bathroom and managed to take a shower in the dirty, cramped wash space. With that done, she set to making breakfast for her son and her father. There wasn't much in her father's kitchen, but she did her best. She made some fried bread, grits, and used up the last five eggs, frying them up in an old skillet.

"What's that you're doing?" her father asked several moments later. "I don't know that I've ever cooked this much in one night in this place." He put water on to boil for coffee, then took the tin of grounds out, measuring them out carefully.

"I got that impression," she said. "But shouldn't a former boxer try to stay in shape? Shouldn't you make sure you take care of yourself?"

"The important word there is *former,*" he said with a chuckle.

They worked together to finish up breakfast and by the time they had the table set, it was nearing 6:30. Jeffrey came into the kitchen, blurry eyes and in the same pajamas he'd worn last night. When the three of them were all in the same room, Ava was reminded of just how cramped the place was. Somehow, she needed to get to the bottom of this mob nonsense. She couldn't allow herself and Jeffrey to live here. Their journey together had started with her father living at *her* place to help with Jeffrey, after all. She'd felt that had been the right move and she needed to get back on that track.

The three of them moved deftly around one another as they all prepared for their day. Roosevelt was out the door by 6:45 to head down to the gym to make sure it was opened up on time. Ava and Jeffrey were out just forty minutes later. They held hands on their way to school and it pained Ava to realize it was the first time she'd spent more than just ten or fifteen minutes with him in the last two days.

"I think we'll go back to our apartment tonight, what do you say?" Ava said as they neared Jeffrey's school.

"Good. Grandpa's bed itches. And it…well, the whole place smells. Don't you think?"

She giggled at this and nudged her son playfully. "Maybe a little bit. But let's not tell Grandpa, okay? I think it might hurt his feelings."

Jeffrey nodded and smiled, looking like he was proud to have a secret to share with his mother—no matter how silly.

When they reached school, Ava gave him a hug and a kiss. He seemed happy enough to do it but when he walked toward the building, she wondered just how much longer that might be the case. He was getting too old, too big, too damned fast. And deep in her heart, she couldn't help but worry that dedicating so much of her time and energy to this new, exciting job might rob them of far too much of their time as he grew up.

She was delighted to see him fall in with two other boys as he neared the front entrance. She could just barely hear him laughing about something, and that was more than enough to warm Ava's heart. She started walking for the precinct, her mind already slipping into work mode. She thought of the Picketts and the Duvalls. She thought of how, despite their often irritable and judging demeanors, none of them were the killer. They had alibis and, more than that, both she and Frank didn't think any of them were capable of murder. More importantly, there was no cause for it among them.

It wasn't Evelyn, nor was it any of the other employees she and Frank had spoken to. No signs of forced entry, no known recent arguments between Penny and anyone—not even any *real* heat from the Duvalls when she'd mentioned wanting to call the wedding to James off.

Well, someone killed the girl, she heard Clarence saying in her head. It was one of those times when his voice was so clear that she could easily imagine him sitting in a comfortable chair in her head, waiting for her to have a chat with him. *Someone killed her, and they're out there, thinking they got away with it.*

It was not the best of thoughts to have as she entered the precinct. The building was already alive with a flurry of activity. There was some casual conversation, some laughter, and a few policemen walking quickly here and there on some errand or another. Wanting to keep a bit of the warmth she'd taken away from Jeffrey's laughter, she thought it might be a good idea to head down to the Women's Bureau to say good morning to Frances and Lottie.

As she made her way to the stairs, though, she saw Frank heading her way from the other side of the bullpen. He had his head lowered and there was the sort of speed in his step that suggested urgency. When he finally looked up to her, he nodded over to the small breakroom at the start of the main hallway. She hurried over to meet him there and they came together right at the front door, thick with the smell of coffee.

"Wimbly, how early *do* you get here?"

He looked annoyed at the question and for a moment, she thought he was going to flat out dismiss it. But then he shrugged and, in a low voice, answered. "If you must know, I meet with Minard twice a week, first thing in the morning, to discuss your performance. I know it seems a little low-brow, but you understand just how much of a risk he's taking to—"

"Yes, I know. And you had that meeting this morning?"

"I did."

"Did it go bad? Is that why you're walking through the building like a man on a mission?"

"No. That's because Minard received another complaint about us. It came in last night on his personal line at home."

"The Picketts?" she said. She already knew the answer, though she could hardly believe it.

"The Picketts," he confirmed. "Now, George Pickett did apparently give us at least some respect and stated that he appreciated what we were trying to do, but he did not want us to come by, bothering him again. He claimed we were overstepping our bounds. He also said he did not want a woman officer on the case."

The spike of anger that tore through her eliminated any of the warmth remaining in her heart. For a very cold and sordid moment, she almost wanted to wash her hands of it and let the son of a bitch go through the remainder of his life without knowing who killed his daughter. Let him deal with it on his own.

"So I'm done with it?" she asked, stemming her anger as well as she could.

"Not just yet. Minard has given us one more day—today—to work on it. But at five o' clock this afternoon, we're off the case."

"With no leads or anyone helpful to answer questions?"

Frank nodded and she was at least glad to see that he looked just as upset as she was about it all. "We're just going to have to go with the crumbs we have. So if you have any desperate measures, now is the time to go ahead and use them."

She did have a very extreme measure in mind. In fact, Ava was almost chilled with how easily it came to her. She nodded and said, "Yeah, I think I have one or two."

"Heading to your jazz clubs?" It wasn't a taunt, but it also didn't sound very hopeful.

"No. Something else." An image of William "Willie" Snide popped up in her head and she hated that it made a messed-up sort of sense that she'd think of going to him again. After all it had been his sadistic insights that had started her on the right path toward the hatchet killer. Maybe he'd be able to help here, too.

"You want me to drive you wherever you have in mind?"

"No, not this time," she said. "I think this is something I might need to do alone." What she meant, though, was: *No way in hell am I going to let you know that I'm going to visit a mass murderer that even my husband thought was out of his mind.*

With that, Ava hurried back to the doors less than five minutes after she'd walked through them. And though the morning sun was already blazing, the thought of sitting across from Willie Snide again kept her feeling cold even as she hailed a cab and slid inside.

CHAPTER TWENTY

The guards at the county jail apparently remembered her from the last visit. It had only been a handful of days ago and she assumed there weren't many people that came to meet Willie. She wasn't sure if it was the same guard that greeted her or not, but he got to his feet right away and nodded politely when she showed her badge and requested to see Willie Snide.

"Gold, right?" the guard asked.

"That's right. Were you here the last time I visited?"

"No, ma'am. But I read about you in the paper. Your husband was a cop, too. And just last week, you caught that hatchet killer, right?"

It was the first time anyone had ever spoken to her as if she was someone famous. It was an odd feeling, odder still that the guard—just a few years younger than she was by the looks of it—seemed to be going a little red in the face in her presence. He also didn't bother to ask why in God's good name she was here to see Willie Snide. He simply led her past the front desk and then asked an assistant to ring the warden because Detective Ava Gold was here to see Snide.

She was then led to the exact same room in which she'd spoken to Willie Snide the first time. It was cold and featureless with only a scarred wooden table adorned with two chairs. She took one of the chairs as the guard gave her one final appreciative glance and closed the door behind him. Just before it snapped completely closed, the guard said, "Snide will be here in a bit."

Ava wasn't quite sure how to feel that she wasn't uneasy about meeting with him. He had unnerved her the first time, sure, but there had been something almost civil about him. He'd not been the salivating, screaming lunatic she'd assumed he would be, not the madman Clarence had described him as. Of course, the acts he'd carried out during his murderous spree several years ago spoke of pure lunacy but she did not fear him based on their previous interactions.

That did change a bit when the door opened several minutes later and Snide was led in. The same bashful guard was escorting him along with another guard that looked as if he might be made of solid brick. It was this guard that was leading Willie along, though when his eyes fell on Ava, he seemed not to even notice either of the guards.

"My God, It's Detective Gold," he said. His amusement and delight seemed totally genuine as the bigger guard practically shoved him down into the chair and then quickly snapped one end of a set of handcuffs to Willie's wrist and the other to one of the legs of the table.

"Want me to stay in here, ma'am?" the large guard asked.

"No, I think we'll be fine."

He seemed taken aback by this, eyeing Willie Snide suspiciously. He then gave a nonchalant shrug and headed for the door. "Just yell if you need me, ma'am." With that, he and the other guard walked out and closed the door.

Once again, for the second time in about a month, Ava was alone with Willie Snide. As they sized one another up, the list of his brutal acts went through her mind—how he'd chewed into the neck of one of his victims, how he'd strung a man up and basically disemboweled him as he removed his organs and labelled them. And in the courtroom, the only remorse he'd shown was that he hadn't discovered how much he enjoyed the act of murder earlier in his life.

"I assume our conversation last time was of some help," Willie said. "Either that or you're desperately attracted to me." He laughed at his own little joke; it was one of the creepiest sounds Ava had ever heard.

"It *was* a big help. I won't lie about that."

"So you caught the killer?"

"We did."

He stared at her, unblinking as he rubbed at his face with his free hand. "Can I assume there's another killer now? And you can't find him?"

"That's correct. And we…I'm sorry. Could you please stop staring at me like that?"

Willie blinked wildly, as if he hadn't had any idea he'd been staring. "So sorry. I'm just trying to decide if you are helpless or inherently smart. To call upon a killer in order to get insights into *another* killer. You'd think more cops would take this route. But then again, I suppose cops aren't known for admitting when they need help, now are they?" He chuckled again and added: "You must be a very special cop indeed."

Special, not so much, she thought. *Inexperienced is more along the right word.*

"This current case has me on a ticking clock," she said. "And yes, I would very much appreciate your help."

"Well, of course. It was a great deal of fun last time just to use my brain for something other than the endless stream of reading and recalling past memories that I've been doing here. And it's not like I get many visitors." He smiled at her, but she was quite sure there was something else behind that smile. She was waiting for him to give her a condition, but it never came. She wondered if he might be saving up his favors for some other time. The idea of it made a scary sort of sense to her and it made her very nervous.

"A sixteen-year-old girl was killed in her bedroom. We don't know for certain, but it appears that she was strangled. She comes from a very wealthy family and from what my partner and I can tell, no one in the family did it, nor did their close friends."

Willie nodded, as if signaling for her to keep going. When he realized that was all he was going to get, he started to shake his head. "If that's all you have, I'm afraid I can't help you. Did this girl have a lover?"

"No, but there was young man she had been promised to and—"

"Yes, that's no good. You see, Detective Gold, all of my murders were out of some dark, malicious need. They were violent, deliberate, and mostly targeted. What it sounds like you're dealing with is something almost accidental…maybe a crime of passion or even hatred. Something based on pure emotion and without any real forethought. If she was pretty, maybe it was out of envy or fear. Either way, it is not something I can identify with." He considered something for a moment and then added: "*Was* she pretty?"

"From pictures I saw in the home, she did look quite attractive."

"What about money? Was her family poor? Wealthy?"

"Wealthy."

"So then perhaps money could have been the reason." He smiled wanly, as if he had not a single care in the world. "When you add money to just about anything, it makes it so much more complicated, doesn't it? He spoke as if he were a philosopher and God help her, Ava thought it made sense. She tried to think of any further details she could give him without identifying the family or giving any names, but came up with nothing.

"I do have to say, though," Willie went on, "that I would truly like to help with this one. "Killing someone so young is a truly despicable act."

"That's where you draw the line?" Ava asked, unable to keep the comment in. She found herself almost wanting to apologize for saying it.

"You seem shocked I have morals of any kind. But yes, that would be where I draw the line. Killing children is the lowest thing a human being can do. They've not yet had a chance to really experience life to its fullest. To take that away is monstrous."

Ava felt herself wanting to debate him on this, to suggest that maybe the nine people he'd killed (in rather grisly fashion, at that) may not yet have really experienced life. And if they hadn't, now that chance was gone. But she had no time for that and, quite frankly, didn't think a man like Willie Snide deserved the opportunity to wax poetic on such things.

"You look disappointed," Willie said. "I'm so very sorry I was not as helpful this time."

"It's not up to you to solve these crimes," Ava said, getting to her feet. "And I need to understand that it is always a mistake to even think of coming to you with—"

"The money aspect changes it all," Willie said, interrupting her. "Is the family kind, or do they sort of look down on people?"

"They are always looking down."

Willie smiled, as if some point he'd been snooping around had been proven. "Ah, and that makes you feel like an outcast on this case, yes? Do they make you feel less than? Like you're unwelcome?"

"Yes, like I don't belong. My partner and I both."

"And there you go." Willie clapped his hands together and chuckled. "The way they make you feel, how many others do you think feel the same way in their presence. You mentioned earlier that you feel confident the family and their friends are all innocent and that is, honestly, probably true. So then….ask yourself another question. Don't ask yourself about the people that *belong* there. Ask yourself—"

"Who *doesn't* belong." Even as she said it, Ava felt there was absolutely something there. With all of the people coming in and out for the party, surely there was someone that could have snuck in under the guise of helping. But between her and Frank, all of the comers and goers had been questioned, from the seamstress to the baker in charge of the cakes and pastries.

So then who did we miss?

"There you go," Willie said. "I see you've come to—"

"Goodbye, Mr. Snide."

She felt rude, cutting him off like that after he'd led her to what she felt might be an important trail of thought. She exited through the door without even looking back at Willie or paying the guard much attention. She thought of people milling about the house that simply might not belong. Maybe not even people *in* the house, but those out on the streets coming and going…

And in a flash, her mind turned to the moment she and Frank had been investigating the old fire escape on the backside of the Picketts' home. They'd been distracted by a scene out in the street as a few wealthy Fifth Avenue-type men had been mocking a poorer man—a man that, now that Ava thought it, may have been a vagrant.

What business did he have out on Fifth Avenue? she wondered. When they'd come across him, she'd been so astounded by the brazen attitudes of the rich men, she hadn't thought to even question why the man being mocked and bullied would even be there at all.

And maybe that had been part of his plan.

Ava rushed through the prison, towards the front doors, barely stopping to thank the guards—and not noticing the one that was so enamored with her even though he was waiting by the front door. No, her mind was already back on Fifth Avenue, where she thought she had a pretty good place to start looking.

CHAPTER TWENTY ONE

She found Frank back at the precinct, which was no big surprise. The surprise came in *where* she found him. He had headed downstairs to the Women's Bureau. There, he was speaking to Lottie and another woman Ava had never gotten to know during her brief time in the downstairs WB headquarters.

When Ava entered the room Lottie gave an exaggerated gasp of surprise. "My, oh my," she said, putting on a bit of dramatic flair. "If it isn't the absolute best of us simple minded women! Hail, my Queen!"

"That's…well, that's just a tad bit much," Ava said, though she could not contain her smile. She looked to Frank and said, "Funny seeing you down here."

"I'm sure it is. But I was hoping to get a word with Frances and she's not here. So I had to make do with Lottie."

"And damn aren't you lucky for it," Lottie said, batting her eyes. "Silly old dick. Anyway, yes, *Detective* Gold. Your partner here was asking me about local bakers and seamstresses in the city. Because *of course* a woman is going to know those things, right?"

"Any lead or reason?" Ava asked, politely ignoring Lottie's chipper little mood.

"Shooting in the dark," Frank said. "I figured maybe I could talk to competing bakers or seamstresses to see if there's bad blood between them and the Picketts. Or them and their rival businesses."

"Good thinking, but I think I may have another approach. But it does mean going back to the Pickett house."

"My God, Gold…are you *trying* get George Pickett to kill you?"

Ava shrugged. "Hey, we've only got the rest of today before we're pulled off the case. I can risk having to arrest the man for assaulting a cop under these circumstances."

"Aww, look at the two of you," Lottie said cheerfully. "Why, you're almost like legitimate partners.

"Almost," Ava said. Then, to Frank, she said: "You do the driving, I'll do the talking."

"If you think it's wise…sure. Let's go."

They both gave their thanks to Lottie as they headed out. They rushed up the stairs as Ava did her best to explain her new theory and line of thought to Frank. Just like last time, she made no mention of going to see Willie Snide.

"I was thinking of the vagrant-type we saw on the street, being harassed by those rich men. I was so blinded by the anger over the men thinking they were better than him that I didn't even question why the man was there in the first place."

"I did," Frank said. "I figured he was just on Fifth Avenue trying to find a job. Something demeaning like washing cars or shining shoes. It's not too uncommon. Based on what we saw, though, I think it takes a special kind of bravery."

They'd made it out to the street now, and Ava saw that Frank had opted to park the patrol car they'd been using directly on the street. They clambored in and Ava was a little shocked by how natural it already felt. She was equally surprised by how fluidly Frank started the engine and weaved flawlessly out into the street. Suddenly, and with just the smallest bit of sorrow, she wondered if Clarence had ever had the privilege of driving a car while on patrol. If he *had*, he'd never mentioned it to her or Jeffrey—and it seemed like the sort of thing he would have *surely* told Jeffrey about.

"Maybe it doesn't even have to be a vagrant or anyone poor, just wandering around Fifth Avenue," she said. "I'm trying to think of someone that seemed like they *might* belong but simply didn't. Like the man we rescued from being harassed by those rich men. He wasn't causing any real trouble, but he just didn't seem to *fit.*"

"Do you really think George Pickett is going to talk to you again after lodging yet another complaint?"

"If he wants to find out who killed his daughter, he's going to have to."

"I'll stress that after today, someone new will be assigned to the case," Frank said. "I'm sure he'd love that but when I express that whoever comes on to replace us is going to have to start from the beginning, I think that'll do it."

Ava leaned forward in her seat, as if willing the car to go faster. She was beginning to appreciate every instance when she and Frank seemed to be connecting. It was already a drastic change from just a few short weeks ago when Minard had decided to pair them together. She wasn't quite sure which part of their journey had helped to show her that she was capable of doing this job (and doing it well) but she was grateful for it.

They pulled up along a surprisingly empty curb in front of the Pickett home just ten minutes later. Ava didn't hesitate in the slightest when she knocked on the door. She rapped loudly, hoping to translate some urgency into it. The door was answered almost right away. When poor, poor Evelyn saw them, she shook her head in dismay.

"I'm not trying to get in trouble with the law or nothing, but I don't know if I should let you two in here."

"It's urgent, Evelyn," Ava said.

"Is it, really? Mr. Pickett is awful mad, and—"

Ava stepped forward, pushing the door open wider. Evelyn, still holding on to it, staggered back a bit. She lowered her head, stepped behind the door as they entered, and didn't say another word. Ava didn't bother asking where George was. She could hear his voice coming from down the large hallway to her right—in the direction of his office.

She and Frank headed in that direction, side by side. Ava was very aware that they were technically intruding and that it would almost certainly result in yet another complaint called in to Minard. But she was shocked to find that she didn't care; she was more concerned with finding Penny's killer. It was a strange feeling, not being too concerned with the fate of her own career. It made her appreciate that risks and decisions had to be made to effectively do this job. It made her respect Frank even more, and it have her a whole new level of appreciation for what Clarence had dealt with.

She could sense Frank moving in a way to cut her off at the office door, so she sped up a bit. She wanted to be the one to knock, to let George Pickett know she could not be intimidated so easily. She knocked on the door, though it was already open, and then stepped inside.

George was sitting behind his desk, speaking to a man that was situated on the opposite side. When George saw Ava standing in his doorway, he looked confused at first but anger quickly dissolved it away. He got to his feet and pointed an accusing finger at her as if he were holding a gun.

"Get the hell out of my house! How many complaints do I need to make?"

"We understand your complaints," Ava said. "But I think you should know that we have a promising lead." She realized this was a bit of an overstatement, but he didn't need to know that. "If you could answer just a few questions, we could—"

"See this man right here?" George said, redirecting his finger to the man sitting at his desk. "This is the director of the funeral home that will be handling Penny's funeral service. I can't even get through *this meeting* without the two of you interfering! Now, if I—"

"Sir, do you *want* to find you daughter's killer?" Ava asked.

"Of course I want to! How dare you even think I—"

"Is it going to be the absolute worst thing if a woman detective plays a part in finding her? Because if so, keep playing it like this. Your complaints have resulted in this being the final day Detective Wimbly and I are able to search for your daughter. And if we're taken off the case, you'll get another detective to help. But that means you'll start all over, from the first step. And it's quite clear you don't like being interrupted. So I suggest you take the time out of your day to hear us out and answer our questions. I can also tell you that the longer the killer is out there, the better chance he has of getting away with it." She took a breath, surprised at how calm she was after having said it all. "Now…would you please take five minutes to answer our questions?"

The funeral director looked as if he'd been pinned to his chair, looking back and forth between the detectives and George Pickett. George, meanwhile, looked like he may have been shot in the chest. He was immobile, his mouth gaping open. It was abundantly clear that he was not used to being talked to in such a way.

"What questions do you have?" he asked. His voice was soft and constrained. It made Ava think he may have responded differently if there wasn't a third party in the room.

"In the day or so leading up to the day of the party and Penny's death, can you think of anyone you may have seen out on the streets or even milling about your house? Someone that just didn't seem to fit into the picture? Someone that didn't belong there?"

"Well, as you very well know, and as I have told you countless times, we had many people in and out of the house, people helping prepare for the festivities. So, there's no way I can answer that."

"Get the party out of your mind," Frank said, speaking just as calmly as Ava. "Think of anyone you may have seen or even interacted with in the days leading up to it."

George started to think a bit deeper. Ava could see the shift in him as he finally made the painstaking decision to actually cooperate with the police. Slowly, something like acknowledgement dawned in his eyes. He stepped around the desk, nodding slowly but still looking off into the distance like he was drawing a memory out of hiding.

"I'll be damned," he whispered. "Now that I think of it, I *did* have words with a man out on the street. This was just as the Duvalls were arriving. I met them out on the porch to have a word with them about the party—a bit of news about some surprises that I didn't want Penny to know about. There was a man out on the street, a black man who very clearly did not belong there. Maybe an immigrant as far as I know. He simply did not know his place. I did my best to usher him away and—"

"Was he causing a disturbance?" Ava asked.

"Disturbing all the fine folk on this street, yes."

"By just *being there?*" Ava managed to catch herself before she went off on a rant. "Were tense words exchanged?"

"Yes. I told him to get back to where he came from. That he had no place on this street, and we didn't want any trouble. And he thought it fit to backtalk me. Can you believe it? Said he was welcome to walk wherever he damn well pleased. But by then, like I said, the Duvalls were here. When it was both Mack and I there to scare him off, he went running. But he was griping the whole way, talking to us over his shoulder and all."

"And that was the end of it?" Frank asked.

"Yes. But a damper on the evening, that's for sure. But just for a bit. I nearly called the constable but in the end, we just laughed it off." He chewed on this for a moment and then added: "I hadn't even given it a second thought until this very moment."

"Could you tell us what he looked like?" Frank asked.

Ava knew what was going to come next and prepared herself for it. Apparently, when it came to people of ethnic origin, George Pickett thought he was worlds better than they were. It did not just stop with women or people that did not make as much money as he did.

"Like I said, he was black and derelict. What else do you need to know?"

The sheer racism and classism on display was enough to make Ava's stomach turn. Still, she soldiered on. "Would you say he spoke back to you in a threatening manner?"

"No more so than a man you may cross over a bit of poker, really. He was angry, yes. But I don't think he was angry enough to have truly come at me for a fight."

Ava nodded, somewhat surprised that George Pickett wasn't already set on trying to pin his daughter's murder on an African American man that he clearly felt vastly superior to. And as much as she hated to give him any sort of push to start thinking in that direction, Ava knew she also could not be naïve enough to completely discount the possibility that this man—or even the vagrant she and Frank had seen, or any others like them—may be responsible for Penny's death. It made her think of the fire escape again. Yes, she'd looked it over but the sudden commotion from the street had sidetracked her. And if she was going to give serious consideration to a potential killer coming in from off the streets, the fire escape looked like the only clear route to get into Penny's bedroom unseen.

"Thank you for your time," Ava said.

"You…you only have until the end of the day?" It was the most vulnerable Ava had heard the man since the first time she met him. That, to Ava, was saying a lot given that he'd recently lost his daughter.

"Yes. But that means we still have serval hours." What she did not say was that it would only take a single telephone call to the precinct to fix that. Instead, she headed for the door, anxious to give the fire escape another look.

CHAPTER TWENTY TWO

Ava knew to pull hard on the ladder this time so she didn't spare any effort. She could tell Frank wanted to pull it down for her, but chose to let her have at it. It seemed he was getting to understand her more and more by the second. He did cut in front of her to climb the old iron ladder first, though. She gave him some space and followed behind him. When she neared the top, Frank offered his hand and pulled her up onto the platform. It seemed to sway the slightest little bit as they walked across it.

They walked to the window and found it locked tightly. There were no obvious signs of forced entry. It also looked very clean, no doubt having been wiped down by Evelyn sometime recently.

"Yeah, no one broke into this window," Frank said.

Ava nodded absently, her eyes already focused on something else. At the right end of the iron platform, there was a thin ledge that ran between Penny's bedroom window and the next. The fire escape walkway didn't quite make it all the way to the other window, but the ledge did. The ledge was purely decorative, a flat slab on concrete that descended down into the side of the building in a decorative slant. The ledge itself looked to be about eight inches wide, with the slant running down about a foot or so before it was buried into the brick and wood of the house itself.

"What about *that* window?" Ava asked, pointing to the window at the other end of the ledge.

"What about it?" Frank asked. "No one could get to that without a ladder down below. And if you—"

He stopped here, noticing where she was looking. He joined her at the edge of the platform and shook his head. "No way. No one would be crazy enough to walk across that thing. Especially not at night." He looked down and sighed. "You're talking about at least a twenty-five foot drop."

"The ledge is wide enough, I think," Ava said. She looked at the ledge, then the window once more. Before she was truly aware of what she was doing, she raised her right leg and carried it over the fire escape railing.

"Gold, what the hell are you doing?" Frank said.

"I'm going over there to check that window."

"I can't let you do that! That's insane!"

Ava threw her other leg over and carefully perched on the very edge of the platform. "I fear if you try to stop me now, I may fall."

"You crazy dame! I won't be responsible for this! If you fall…"

"If I fall, you'll no longer be saddled with a crazy dame for a partner. Now be quiet so I can concentrate."

She did her best not to look down as she stepped over empty air and onto the ledge. She knew she had small feet; it was something Clarence had teased her about repeatedly. And now finally, those small feet were going to come in handy. With one foot on the ledge, she reached out and placed her hand against the rough brick that made up the exterior along the back of the Pickett house. Pivoting her weight, she then carried the left foot over. With her entire body now on the ledge, she leaned as tightly against the wall as she could. Her entire foot nearly fit on the ledge, with only the very end of her heel hanging off. She grinned nervously as she tried to imagine herself doing this in heels, but as it was, her Oxfords seemed to handle this risk nicely.

"Jesus wept," Frank said from the platform. "For goodness sake, be careful."

"For goodness sake, *hush!*"

He did, but she could feel his eyes on her and that was somehow just as bad. She did her best to shut him out, leaning ever so slightly forward as she slid her feet along the ledge. It was slow going but she made the first several feet with no problem. She figured if she was a big bosomed broad—perhaps like Frances—there was no way she'd be able to do his. If the ledge were just two inches shorter, she would have likely already fallen. But of course, that was no way to think. She looked down, barely able to move her head without her forehead striking the brick She looked to her feet, to the small piece of the ledge, and continued sliding along.

She was nearly at the end of the ledge when someone on the other side of the house shouted out. It was a shout of joy, of a man running into an acquaintance, but Ava did not realize it right away. All she knew was that it was an unexpected sound, and her body reacted as such. Her hands came off the wall ever so slightly, and her knees buckled just a bit.

Ava felt herself starting to fall backwards. Her heart leaped in her chest and her guts seemed to think she was already plummeting to the Picketts' back lot twenty-five feet below. But her eyes still saw the brick in front of her, focusing and redirecting her panicked brain.

Slowly, she leaned forward. For a split second, she *knew* she was wavering between leaning back to the brick or letting gravity claim her.

She placed one hand on the brick again and the rest of her body seemed to follow that small action. When she was centered again and no longer felt like her heart was going to leap out of her mouth, she inched those last few steps. At the end of the ledge, she looked to the right and saw that the window was installed just like Penny's; there was the slightest of indentations, giving her about six inches more than the ledge. As she found herself stepping out over open air once more, she could not help but wonder: *Why didn't the bastards that built this place just have the fire escape go all the way along the back?*

When she was standing on the window's larger ledge, she had to bend down just the slightest bit. This wasn't quite as dangerous as being out on the ledge because she simply had to lean forward. And if she leaned forward too far, she'd simply slam into the window. And boy howdy, wouldn't George Pickett love that?

She did have to press her forehead against the glass to check to see if the window was locked. She put both hands on either side of the frame and pushed upward. The window slid without any problem. She moved her hands to the bottom of the window, making sure she didn't fall backwards. It took a bit of creative bending, but she was then able to step into the room.

Ava found herself standing in a room that was just a bit smaller than Penny's. A bed sat in the center of the far wall, perfectly made and untouched. A small dresser sat along the wall to the left. Ava checked the drawers and found only a spare change of sheets. With the lack of clothes in the drawers and the pristine nature of the bed, she assumed this was a guest room. She recalled the closed door inside, just beside Penny's bedroom.

The room itself seemed innocent enough. But for that window to offer such easy access, it suddenly became very interesting in terms of the case. If someone were determined enough, they could certainly have taken it upon themselves to inch along that ledge to find a way in.

"Gold?" Frank called from outside. "What did you find?"

"One second," she called, still looking around the room. The only other thing to investigate was a small closet on the right wall. She walked over to it and wasn't surprised to find it empty. What she *was* surprised to find, though, was that there was no wall in the back of it. Instead, it was blocked off by a series of shoes on the floor and several hanging dresses and gowns—all of which she had seen before.

Ava stepped into the closet, took a single step, and pushed the clothes to the side. They slid over on their hangers and revealed Penny Pickett's room. Ava stood there for a while, astounded that they'd missed this the first time.

The closets were connected.

***

"I don't get it," Ava said. "I mean, is this even a normal way to build a house?"

Frank, who had come in the much easier way through the front door and then up the stairs, looked into the guestroom closet and to Penny's bedroom on the other side. "Not sure. I do think that sometimes these older homes did have rooms that were adjoined like this, though. Makes me think this space wasn't always intended as a closet."

"So given the window and the closet…do you think we're finally on to something here?"

"Maybe. Still, it makes me wonder…would the killer have to *know* the walkthrough closet was here? Because if so…"

"If so, it would have to be someone that was familiar with the house, right?"

"Not necessarily. Anyone with enough determination could do exactly what you just did to find their way inside. They'd have to be a little crazy just like you, but I think it's possible."

Ava thought it all over for a moment. She knew she didn't want to bother George Pickett again. If she had her way, they'd not speak to him again until they had his daughter's killer in custody.

"Okay then," she said. "I say we hit the streets. Ask around about the African American man Pickett berated. The people that live around here seem to really get offended when someone not of their own class pops up around. So you'd think if someone else saw this man or had an issue with him, they'd clearly remember it. And if anyone saw him maybe wandering around the Pickett home, especially around the back, that could lead to something."

"Yeah, that's a good point."

They closed the closet door and left the guest bedroom. When they made their way downstairs, they made no attempt to say goodbye to George. They simply gave Evelyn a polite nod as they left the house and made their way back out onto the street. Somehow, it had already come to be 2:30 in the afternoon, and the final day Minard had given them to wrap up the case was quickly dwindling away.

With no other clear course of action to take, they started knocking on the doors of every other home along the same stretch of Fifth Avenue that the Picketts occupied. Most of the doors were answered by maids or servants of some kind. In only two cases was the patriarch of the home available. Both men seemed eager to help but neither of them could recall ever seeing an African American male causing any sort of trouble along the street.

They got their first potential lead after knocking on the door of a furniture shop. The proprietor was an old man that welcomed them in warmly. The shop was more like a workshop with just a small display room set up with rocking chairs, benches, and stools.

"People like that tend to stand out, don't they?" the proprietor asked. He was a tall man with a white beard and shaggy white hair that was tucked mostly under a driver's cap. "And that's why I *do* remember a man just like that. He came by asking for work. Seemed nice enough, no real problems. But he got very belligerent when I told him I wasn't looking for any help. Just a few cross words, nothing terrible."

"Is there anything else you recall about him?" Frank asked. "Maybe the clothes he was wearing or something like that?"

"Well, this has been three days ago, and my mind isn't as sharp as it once was. But I believe he was wearing a dusty grey jacket and a tattered shirt underneath." His eyes grew wide as another detail presented itself. "Oh! And he was carrying a case with him."

"Like a suitcase?" Ava asked.

"No, no…it was much larger than a suitcase. I thought there might be some sort of tools in it. It had a very strange shape to it. I nearly asked him what he was carrying, but honestly I just wanted him out of my shop as soon as possible."

Ava knew that George Pickett had mentioned nothing about a case, but maybe that didn't mean anything. Maybe the case was left somewhere else when the Picketts had their altercation. Or maybe this was just another man altogether. Either way, she felt they needed to find out. Ava and Frank gave their thanks and left the shop.

They tried the grocer next door and had no help there, then went across the street to a small clothing boutique. Ava bristled a bit as she went inside, realizing that no matter how hard she worked and saved up her money, she would likely never be able to realistically afford any of the dresses on display. She and Frank approached the counter in the back where a kindly-looking older lady was thumbing through different fabric samples. She looked up with a bright, white smile.

"How can I help you folks?" she asked. She looked to Frank and said, "You look like a copper. Looking for some new duds?"

"Good eye," Frank said. "I *am* a detective, and this is my partner, Detective Gold."

"Is that so?" she asked, clearly astounded that not only was there such a thing as a female detective, but that she was in her store.

"Yes ma'am," Ava said. "And we're asking around the neighborhood about a man that may be a suspect in a case we're working on. Have you by any chance seen a disheveled-looking African American man in the last few days? He may have been carrying an oddly shaped case with him."

The smile on her face said it all. Yes, she'd seen such a man and yes, she was eager to help. "I *did* see a man just like that. It was two days ago, I believe. He seemed very lost out there on the street and yes, he was carrying a very strange case with him."

"Did you speak to him at all?" Frank asked.

"I did. I walked out and asked if I could help him because, as I said, he did seem lost. Maybe a little out of place. I walked outside and asked if I could help him, and he told me he'd somehow gotten very turned around. He said he was looking for a nightclub, and I sort of laughed. As you know, I'm sure, there aren't many night clubs out this way. But I'd heard of this one, and did my best to give him directions."

"So he was looking for a night club and was carrying a large case?" Ava asked. "Was it an instrument case of some kind?"

"Yes, I believe it was."

"What was the name of the club he was looking for?"

"The Meadowlark."

Frank looked at Ava, slightly excited. "You know it?"

"I never played there, but yes, I know it." She regarded the seamstress and returned the woman's smile. "Thanks so much. You've been a huge help."

They left the shop and Frank immediately checked his watch. "It's already four o' clock," he said. "Where the hell did this day go?"

"I don't know about where the *day* has gone," Ava said, "but you and I are heading to the Meadowlark."

"Isn't it too early for bands to play?"

"Not really. Some get there very early to warm up and jam a bit. Besides, I'm more interested in speaking to the owner."

They hurried back to their car, parked in front of the Pickett residence. As Frank started the engine and pulled out into the street, it comforted Ava to know that somehow, on only her second official case, she was headed back to the jazz clubs she was so comfortable with. And, more importantly, getting the hell away from Fifth Avenue.

CHAPTER TWENTY THREE

The Meadowlark was a newer club, having just opened up not too long before Ava's brief jazz club career came to an end. She'd never performed there but had gone to a single show not too long after it opened. The Meadowlark stood out above most other jazz clubs mainly because of its location. A few blocks to the north of the grittier and often frowned upon clubs, it seemed to possess more charm and drew what would be considered a more respectable crowd.

That's why there were hardly any patrons inside when Ava and Frank arrived there at 4:45 in the afternoon. There were two people sitting at a table drinking coffee and, as Ava had explained, several men on the small stage up front, setting up for the night's gig. Even the interior of the Meadowlark was a step above most of the dives Ava had performed in. The stage was well-designed and served as the central part of the club. The ceilings were high, and the windows along the back wall allowed for lots of natural light to fall on the new, polished wood floors.

Making their way into the mostly empty building, Ava studied the band. There were currently three men on stage; one was setting up a small drum kit, a second was polishing up a trumpet, and a third was opening up a rather large case. It was an African American man and the case was larger than Ava had been picturing in her head. It was a case for a stand-up bass. As he took it out and set it gently on the edge of the stage, Ava knew what came next.

"That's our guy," she said, nodding toward him.

"Yeah, that's a pretty damn big case," Frank said. "Is that a bass?"

"It is," she said, walking closer to the stage. The man had an old but beautiful stand-up. As it sat on the edge of the stage, he went back into the case and she knew what he was going for right away. She watched as he removed the little tin case and popped the cap open. She'd watched many bass players coat their strings with the rosin that typically filled these sorts of tins. She'd even seen some poorer musicians use skin ointments for the same use. But this man was using rosin—a substance that bore a striking resemblance to the smear they'd found on Penny's floor when they'd first searched her room.

"See that stuff he's putting on his strings?" Ava asked.

"Yeah. Is that to make it so that the strings don't wear on his fingers?"

"That, and it makes changing chords a bit easier. But it's also a very likely candidate for that smear of residue we found on Penny's floor."

With that said, Ava hurried to the edge of the stage. The drummer hadn't noticed them yet, but the trumpet player gave them a polite nod. The bass player was halfway through greasing the first string when he noticed them approaching.

"You playing bass tonight?" Ava asked.

"Sure am," the African American man said, delighted. "First time in this place. They say the sound really thumps in here."

"Can I ask what your name is?"

"Sure thing," he said, finishing up the first string. The rosin glistened in the overhead lights. There was the slightest bit of differentiation between it and the smear on Penny's floor but if had been there long enough and dried slightly it would be a very close match. "The name's Robert Abraham, ma'am. Good to meet you."

"Mr. Abraham, were you by any chance over on Fifth Avenue two days ago? Particularly in the afternoon?"

He chuckled and nodded, a man happy and anxious for the gig he was set to play. "Sure was. Some joker gave me terrible directions to this place. I had a try-out two evenings ago, you see? I took a wrong turn somewhere a little bit past here and ended up in that rich, fancy part of the city."

"And did you have words with anyone while you were there?"

Robert Abraham gave them a puzzled look, suddenly not so interested in oiling up his strings. "Hold on, now. Who are you folk, anyway?"

Ava showed her badge. Frank did the same beside her, but Ava was very aware that he was letting her run the lead here. "Detectives Gold and Wimbly, NYPD. Mr. Abraham, we need you to come with us, please."

"Am I under arrest or something?" He chuckled nervously and added: "Won't be the first time I've been arrested for being black."

"Currently, no, you are not under arrest," Ava said. "We just need to ask you some questions about your afternoon on Fifth Avenue."

"Look, I might have had some words with—"

"Not here," Frank said. "We need you to come with us."

"But what about the show?"

Ava felt for the man because she knew the excitement involved with playing a new place. "I guess they're just going to have to find a replacement."

***

Ava was both impressed and a little confused by Robert Abraham's behavior as he sat in the interrogation room. He had not been formally arrested yet and the questioning so far had been limited to the brief exchange back at The Meadowlark. And though he had been taken into custody and robbed of his chance at playing a fairly respected place, he was cooperative and borderline polite.

Ava and Frank had joined him, Frank closing the door behind them. Ava studied Robert for a moment, crossing her arms not as a defensive stance, but as a contemplative one.

"You seem very agreeable," Ava commented. "It makes me think you aren't all that unfamiliar with being in a police station."

"Well, it sure isn't my first time," Robert said. "The shame of it is, the only crime I've ever broken was a bit of gambling and depending on where you're from, that really ain't all that illegal now, is it. But ever since I came here to New York about a year or so ago…yes, I've been arrested a few times. Guilty of being black, I suppose."

"So you've been arrested but never actually placed in jail?" Frank asked.

"That's right. Don't believe I've ever had the pleasure of coming to this particular precinct, though."

"Well, I can assure you that we haven't brought you here because of the color of your skin," Ava said. "It seems you were on Fifth Avenue on the afternoon before a sixteen-year-old girl was murdered. And the only person the father claims to have had a cross word with that did not belong in or near his house was an African American male. Now, while this father did not mention the large case you were carrying, we have two other witnesses that saw you on Fifth during that same day and they both say you were carrying a case—a case I now know was carrying that stand-up bass."

"Any of this sound familiar to you?" Frank asked.

"Oh yeah, it all does. I can clear up the timeline for you there, though. I got directions from an old drummer I used to play with and those directions were just *awful.* So I ended up on Fifth Street, right around six o' clock or so, lugging that bass with me. I stopped by this place that I thought was just someone's workshop but turned out to be a

123

furniture store. Some old guy, building his own furniture and selling it. I thought it was fascinating, so asked if he was looking for help. Well, you would have thought I'd called his momma a bad name, the way he yelled at me. So, I got out of there and figured I better get out of that part of the city as quick as I can. I was out on the street, trying to figure out where I'd made a wrong turn, when this kind old lady from a clothes store came up to me. She told me right where I needed to go."

"And did you head right over to the Meadowlark after she told you how to get there?"

"Sure did. I walked right where she told me to go. But it just so happened that on the way, I made the mistake of passing by one of those types that thinks he owns the city, you know? I didn't look at this man or his wife, and I certainly didn't speak to him. But he yelled at me to get away from his house, to get back where I belonged—whatever that means! And you know…I've been through enough of those situations where I *know* I should have just kept my mouth shut. But it was hard, *too* hard, and I argued right back with him. Told him the city didn't belong to him and I was just passing through."

"Did you ever threaten him in any way?" Frank asked.

"No, sir. Not once. That's pretty much all I said to him. But that was enough. You could tell he was expecting me to be a good, obedient ol' negro and keep walking on. Looked like he was at a loss for words when I dared talk back to him."

"And after that, did you make it to your tryout in time?" Ava asked.

"No, I was late. But as you saw this evening, I made it on with the band anyway."

"But it was just a tryout, not a gig, right?" Ava asked.

"Yes ma'am."

"After the tryout, where did you go? Did you ever head back out to Fifth Avenue?"

"Not at all. I had a coffee with a woman at the club and then made my way back home."

"And where is home, Mr. Abraham?" Frank asked.

"Over on 158th Street. It's a doozy of a walk from there to Fifth, let me tell you."

Ava considered all of this. If his story checked out, there would be plenty of people that could back up the fact that Robert had indeed been to the tryout. But that would do very little to clear him, given that Penny had been killed sometime between eleven at night and nine in the morning. That was ten whole hours that were wide open for pretty much anything to happen.

"Did you go back out to Fifth Avenue later?" Frank asked. "After the tryout, I mean?"

"Lordy, no. I don't agree with those folks telling others to know their place, but I also know that I ain't cut out for that sort of place."

"You're certain about that?" Ava asked.

"Yes ma'am."

"Anyone that can back that story up? A wife, girlfriend, roommate, anything like that?"

"Well, I live with my brother, but he's visiting our father down south, so he wasn't there."

Ava and Frank exchanged a look. Ava wasn't sure Robert Abraham was their guy after all. She tried to gauge Frank's initial feelings, but couldn't get a good read on him.

"Mr. Abraham, I'm going to be truthful with you here," Ava said. "The man that argued with you…his daughter was murdered that same night, right there in his house. We have no leads, and only one clue. There was a smudge of what I thought was grease or oil of some kind on her bedroom floor. I didn't make the connection until today, when I saw you oiling down your strings, that it looked an awful lot like rosin."

Fear seemed to sink into Robert for the first time, but there were equal parts disbelief, too. "I swear to you and to the good Lord above, I never went back to that house!"

"Right now, we have you at the scene earlier in the day, having an argument with the father. You even said yourself that it's a part of town you don't go to often, so it seems even odder that you'd be there."

"I told you—"

"Yes, the bad directions," Frank interrupted. "I know. Look, for now, we need you to stay here. We need to get a look at the rosin you're using for your strings. And we also need to try to piece together your whereabouts between when you left the club after having coffee and when your day started the following morning."

"It's not me," Robert said diligently. "And because it's easier to pin a crime on a poor black man, I'm going to miss a big gig. That's not right." He levelled his eyes toward Ava and added: "And you know it."

"We'll have someone head back to the Meadowlark to retrieve your tin of rosin," Frank said.

Ava only nodded in agreement as she headed out of the interrogation room. When she was back out in the hall, she walked slowly to the bullpen. She looked in the direction of Captain Minard's office, knowing full well that all they'd heard from Robert Abraham was going to be more than enough for Minard to go ahead and have them make a formal arrest. The case for the arrest would be thin, but she wasn't stupid or naïve; she knew that Robert's skin color and Pickett's apparent dislike of him would make it a stronger case.

"Want to go tell Minard?" Frank asked.

"No."

"Well, we sort of have to. It's our job and all."

"It's not him. That argument wasn't nearly enough to cause someone to kill. Even Pickett said it wasn't much of an altercation."

"Gold, I've seen people commit murder over much less than the argument between the two of them. I'm sure Clarence did, too."

Ava winced. She still wasn't used to anyone mentioning Clarence when she was at work—especially Frank. She ignored this for the moment and added: "Did you see his feet?"

"What?" Frank asked, baffled by the question.

"His feet. They were pretty big—much bigger than mine. For him to inch his way across the ledge, he'd have to be an acrobat or something."

Frank sighed, looking back to Minard's office. "Fine. We'll make sure to include that in the report. Now come on. For right now, making an arrest is all we need."

He started for Minard's office and Ava reluctantly followed. She didn't like Frank's approach of *making an arrest is all we need*. More than that, she also thought there might be more hesitation in Frank, and certainly in the decision Minard was about to make, if Robert Abraham were a white man.

Still, she followed behind Frank as they went to speak to Minard where they'd have a discussion that she was worried might ruin the life of an innocent man.

CHAPTER TWENTY FOUR

To his credit, Minard listened closely as Frank and Ava explained how the afternoon had gone. He sat idly behind his desk as they sat on the other side. He didn't interrupt a single time, but Ava could imagine him already anxious to be on the telephone, wiring George Pickett to let him know they'd made an arrest.

Ava let Frank do most of the talking because she had no delusion about Minard seeing her as Frank's equal just yet. She was relieved when Frank skipped right over the part of the story where she went balancing along the back of the Picketts' home, leaving it to a simple trip up a fire escape. She remained quiet through most of it, opting to become more vocal when it came time to point out a few of the flaws in a theory she'd hoped would close the case just an hour and a half ago.

"There are a few things that make me doubtful," Ava said. "First of all, how would he have known the rooms were connected?"

"I don't see why it would have mattered," Minard said. "All he had to do was go out into the hallway and find Penny in the next room. For all we know, he never even opened the closet."

Ava internally scolded herself. Of course that was a possibility. Anyone that had passed through the closet would have surely knocked some of Penny's shoes askew. But it had been neat and clean, everything perfectly organized.

"Also," she said, already sensing that she was fighting a losing battle, "there's no way we can know for sure it was rosin we saw in the floor. And the more I think about it, the less it makes sense. Rosin isn't something he would have had on him. Even if he had his tin of it, it would have been in his pocket. It makes no sense for it to have been on the floor."

Minard rubbed at his head and gave Ava an incredulous look. "Why are you trying to poke holes in your own case?"

"After speaking with him, I just don't think it's him."

"Please, Gold….don't tell me this is because you're sympathizing with him because he's a jazz musician."

"No, sir. But the way he spoke, the way he told us all that happened on the afternoon he got lost…I believe him."

"Frank, what do you think?"

Frank thought about it for several moments. He removed his hat and scratched nervously at his hair. "I think we have him on the scene less than six hours before she could have been killed. I think we have him exchanging cross words with the father, and a substance on the floor that bears a striking resemblance to the same material he puts on his bass strings." He gave Ava an apologetic look and said, "I think he's our guy."

"Then make the arrest."

Ava found herself biting at her lip to not say anything she'd regret. After a few seconds of reeling herself in, she finally let out a simple comment. "We're making a mistake."

Before Frank could be swayed, Minard waved him out. "Go on, Frank. Make the arrest and I'll let you be the one to make the call to Pickett. Ava…while he does that, stay here, would you? I'd like a word."

She'd just started to get up from her chair, but eased herself back into it. She looked across the desk at Minard as Frank left the office and closed the door behind him. One thing she was quickly starting to understand about Minard was that it was hard to get a read on him. As she sat there and waited for him to speak, she had no idea if he was going to praise her for her critical thinking on the case or chew her out because of her newfound doubts.

"You know," he said, "Clarence had a soft heart, too. It was one of the things I really liked about him. He was the kindest man I've likely ever met. But he didn't let that kindness interfere with his job. I think what you're doing right now is showing your sympathetic side. I can tell you right now that nine times out of ten, your gut reaction is the right one."

"I appreciate all of that," Ava said. "But there are too many questions for me now. Just speaking to him, he doesn't seem like the sort of man to—"

"Gold, I gave you one more day to get this thing wrapped and you worked hard to get it done. You're driven and determined, and that's what's going to endure. That's what's going to make you an excellent detective. I can already see traces of it." He got to his feet and slowly walked to the door. He placed his hand on the knob, and before opening he looked to her with all sincerity. "You did a damned fine job today, Gold. Don't beat yourself up over this. If for some reason Robert Abraham *isn't* the right man, it'll be proven in court."

He then opened the door and stood there, his unspoken way of telling her that they were done here. Ava excused herself, not quite sure how to feel about the brief conversation. On the one hand, it was great to hear Minard sing Clarence's praises and to even compare her to him in some ways. But she also couldn't help but pick up on an almost lackadaisical attitude about putting Robert Abraham behind bars. It was almost as if Minard—and even Frank, to some degree—were fine with getting the arrest down in the books rather than making sure they had the right man. She supposed a lot of it came down to George Pickett's pestering. The sooner they could please him with an arrest, the sooner they were done with him and his constant complaints about every damn thing.

Just before Minard closed the door, she stopped and turned back to face him. "Sir, can I get your permission to continue investigating?"

"No, Gold. Frank is making the arrest, and the case is going to be closed quite soon."

"Fine. The arrest will be made and Pickett will rest a bit easier. But what if I continue to work on it in the background?"

"No, Gold. And this is the last time I'm going to be polite about it."

With that, he closed the door. Ava stood there for a moment, rattled by the feeling that her push to close the case and her overall thoroughness may have just condemned an innocent man. Surely, there had to be *something* she could do.

As she made her way through the bullpen, she looked back to the direction of the interrogation rooms. Frank would be in the second one, reading Robert Abraham his rights. Maybe there was a very small chance he was the killer. Maybe he'd been so enraged by George Pickett's prejudice that he snapped and decided to revisit the house, break in through the guest room window, and strangle Penny Pickett. It didn't feel right to her, but she had to at least consider it as a possibility.

A flimsy and unlikely possibility, but a possibility.

She made her way to the front of the building, suddenly anxious to get out of the building, to be by herself to try to figure this all out. She left the precinct without leaving a message for Frank, her mind already scrambling for some way to help free a man she was now quite certain was totally innocent of the crime her partner was currently arresting him for.

CHAPTER TWENTY FIVE

Her thoughts were so muddled and frantic that she didn't realize that she'd never made a firm decision on whether or not to stay another night at her father's apartment until she was walking in through the front doors of her apartment building. Her father and Jeffrey would be back over at the gym, either closing the place up or scrounging around the apartment for something for dinner.

She nearly stopped right there in the lobby but figured that while she was here, she may as well go upstairs to grab some food for dinner and even a shower in her own bathroom. And as they ate dinner, they'd discuss what it would look like to all come back here. She was even starting to wonder if she could just convince her father to live here with them. That apartment over the boxing gym *did* fit his vibe and lifestyle, but it was also a dump. The trick would be convincing him this was true.

Ava walked up the stairs, her thoughts still wrapped around the unfortunate image of Frank reading Robert Abraham his rights. She wondered if Robert was in a holding cell yet. She wondered if anyone had gone out to the Meadowlark to get the bass and the rosin yet. This all rattled around in her head as she came to her door. She unlocked it, stepped inside paused for a moment.

Maybe it was just because she was still a little haunted by what she'd found waiting for her the last time she'd arrived home, but something felt different. She couldn't quite place what it was…maybe something in the air, some smell or…

What is it? she asked herself. She tried to tell herself it was nothing, that she was just being paranoid. But as she slowly stepped through the kitchen and into the den, she saw the glass on the floor. The window in the den had been shattered. The entire bottom pane had been busted out. Ironically, it was the window that looked out to the little ledge on the side of the fire escape that snaked its way up the building. Avoiding the broken glass, she looked around the room to see if anything had been disturbed. It all looked as it should for the most part, though she could see where some of the glass had been unnaturally scattered, brushed a bit forward away from the rest. It looked as if a single foot had passed through it as someone advanced through the apartment.

Ava drew her sidearm, still not used to the feel of it. It felt like a rock in her hand, like something she was not ready to use in any real capacity. She checked the place over thoroughly, pausing at every corner and pivoting around to make sure there was no one lying in wait. It was another indicator to her that, even though she already had the job of detective and the skills of an above-average boxer, she really did need to get some proper training.

She searched the rest of the apartment in this same way and found it empty. She ended the search back in the den, looking down to the glass. Of course, it could have been any random thief…but she could not see where anything had been taken or defaced in any way. Given that, she was quite sure she knew what had caused this; it had been done by the same people that had left a rat on her doorstep.

She'd had quite enough of this. And when it mixed with the grief she felt over getting Robert Abraham unfairly arrested, it started to boil up within her. With a scowl on her face, Ava stormed out of her apartment, making sure to holster her sidearm before leaving.

Maybe she couldn't fix the mistake she'd made with Robert Abraham, but she could sure as hell do something about the people that continued to harass her.

***

Night had only just properly fallen when Ava made her way back out onto the streets. She had a clear destination in mind but had to stop here and there at intersections to make sure she remembered how to get there. As she walked briskly through the streets, passing by the occasional cluster of pedestrians, she started to understand that the city was a different place at night. In some areas, things felt more relaxed— as if the city itself was unwinding after a long day. But she also knew this meant the dangers in some of the worst parts of the city would be even worse.

She kept this in mind as she made her way to her destination. She was certain she was about to make a mistake, but managed to look past it. The only reason she had any doubt at all was because of Jeffrey; if she ended up dead or even somehow in jail, Jeffrey was going to have a long stretch ahead of him as he was raised by his grandfather. It was *almost* enough to make her change her mind—to just go to the gym and join them for a miserable dinner. But by the time this even crossed her mind, she was almost there. The streets were starting to look familiar, made even more familiar by the darkness of night.

And then, as she came to a sleepy intersection, she saw it: the automobile dealership where she'd first met and promptly arrested Tony Two. It was the site of where her troubles with the mob had started, so she figured it might be a suitable place to visit to see what she could do to end those same troubles. Her hope was that because the mob was so full of itself and did, in many ways, have a deadly grip on the city, that they'd return to their favorite gambling backroom even though it had been busted up by the police less than two weeks ago.

As she came to the back of the lot, she saw that her hunch was apparently correct. There were three Fords parked behind the building. Just several feet away from those automobiles was the door that led to the backroom where she's disrupted a poker game just several days ago (though, by now, it felt like months had already passed).

She reached for her sidearm as she neared the back door, no longer Clarence's tried and true Colt, but now a department-issued Smith and Wesson .38. But just as her hand was hovering over the butt, she removed it. She'd not only been instructed by Minard to only draw it if her life or the life of her partner was in danger, but she also knew that if she marched in there with a gun in her hand, her son would very likely wake up tomorrow morning with no parents. And Lord only knew it was going to be hard enough for him without a father.

So then what the hell are you doing here? she asked herself.

She thought of the broken window, of the bloodied rat at her door. She could see where the door had been repaired since she'd last visited and found it almost ironic that she was about to head back in.

This time, though, she figured she'd try something a little different. She approached the door and gently knocked three times. She then moved quickly to the edge of the door, where it would swing open when someone answered. Assuming a boxer's stance and drawing her right arm back tightly to her chest, she waited. It took about ten seconds before anyone came to the door. When they did, the door was opened just a bit, just enough for the person on the other side to look out to see who had knocked. This was exactly what Ava expected. She waited until the door stopped moving and drove her right fist forward quickly and with spot-on accuracy.

She barely saw the man on the other side of the door before her fist took him right on the point of his chin. As he stumbled backwards, Ava reached out and grabbed him by the collar of his shirt. She then wheeled him around hard enough to nearly make him stumble but then drew him closer to her. When she felt him struggling against her, she delivered a left-handed jab into his ribs at the same moment she kicked the door behind her and slid inside the back room. She held him close to her, using him as a shield and peering over his shoulder into the room.

As she'd expected, there was a poker game in progress. There were only three other men sitting around the table, and none of them were Tony Two. Two of them had drawn their guns, while the third sat frozen at the table, not quite sure what was happening.

"Damn it all," one of the armed mobsters said. "You're that Ava Gold broad!"

"That's right. And I need to know who you fellas work for."

The other armed man stepped forward, levelling his gun at her. He was of average height and looked well-built under the button-down shirt and sport coat he wore. "You're out of your pretty little mind. I think maybe we bump you and take your dead body to the bosses."

"Not so fast," the other armed man said. "This ain't some normal skirt. She's a cop, and she's been in the papers lately. Kill her and the heat will come down on us for sure."

The man in her grip continued to fight against her. To keep him still, she pushed him forward a bit and brought her knee up into the small of his back. He crumpled like a piece of paper as he hit the floor. Confident in what the first armed man had said, Ava left him there and raised her hands in the air.

"I'm not here to fight. I just need to talk to someone higher up your little ladder."

"What gives you the right?" the second armed man asked.

"The dead rat and the broken window at my apartment for starters."

The armed man in the sport coat gently sat his gun down in the poker table, knocking over a little pile of chips as he did so. "I'll tell you what," he said, with a grin. He then gave her what Clarence once referred to as "the ol' up-down"—essentially devouring her with his eyes. She almost didn't care because this damned policewoman's outfit was horrendous. "You put your dukes up and fight me. You come out on top, I'll march you to the boss myself."

"Hold on now, Billy," the man still sitting at the table said. "Haven't you read the papers about this d—"

"No way in hell a dame beats me," Billy said.

"And if I lose?" Ava said, a smile on her face.

"If you lose, we may just strip you outta that uniform and see what's underneath. And you're probably gonna be walking funny when you go back home."

Ava nodded and stepped to the side to allow them more room to fight. "That's a fair deal she said. "No guns, no piling up on me."

"Oh, sweet thing, I won't need any help."

And with that, Billy came forward. He took a quick, lumbering stride that took Ava by surprise. When he brought the haymaker around, she knew she'd not have time to fully duck it so she brought her arms up in a defensive gesture. His fist pummeled the meat just below her wrist and the impact of it made her stagger backwards. Her forearm throbbed from the impact and started to cramp.

Billy was coming forward again, this time taking a street-brawler stance. He threw out a quick left-handed jab that Ava easily swatted away. He then went for a rib shot which she also swatted away. She was biding her time, waiting for her arm to loosen up as she led him around the table. She blocked yet another shot as he threw a jab at her face. Feeling her arm finally loosening up, Ava threw a hard jab to his chest. He blocked it, but barely. And it had been what she expected. At the same time that he blocked her right hand, she brought her left hand around and slammed it into the side of his head. As his head rocked hard to the right, she used her right hand to grab the back of his head and then drove two quick, successive left-handed jabs into his face.

Billy staggered, but did not fall. In fact, he came forward again, throwing a lazy but brutal right-handed swing. Ava sidestepped it easily and then caught his arm by the elbow. She bent it hard to the left, and Billy cried out, dropping to his knees. With his face so close to her legs, Ava hated to waste the opportunity. She drove her right knee up, slamming it into his chin. There was an almost musical *click* and then, after swaying almost comically for about two seconds, Billy went to the ground.

Ava placed her right hand over her sidearm and looked to the other two men. "Are we going to have any problems?"

The man at the table shook his head slowly. The other armed man placed his gun on the poker table right beside his fallen friend's. "No problem," he said.

"Now, which of you is going to take me to your boss? It seems Billy isn't in any shape to drive."

CHAPTER TWENTY SIX

It was a tense drive, to say the least. Ava ordered both of the remaining men to sit in the front. Through little spats of conversations Ava had picked up as they talked to one another, she ascertained that the man that had remained seated through the entire exchange was called Tack and the second was Vin, which Ava assumed was short for Vinnie. As they sat in front, Ava sat in the back of Vin's car with her Smith and Wesson drawn and sitting on her lap. She'd told them she'd put a hole in either of them if they tried anything funny and it seemed that they believed her. This was a relief, because she still wasn't quite sure she'd ever be able to actually shoot anyone if it came down to it.

The drive was surprisingly short. It was just a few streets to the east, toward what she'd always thought of as the business district. There, Vin guided his car into the parking lot of a restaurant that looked a bit more elegant than others in the area. Even from the outside, it looked prestigious by just the way the glass kept the lights inside looking muted and mysterious.

Vin drove around to the side of the restaurant, parking alongside a few other cars. She assumed this was the employee lot. There were a few trashcans and crates hidden away from the street and the primary parking lot. Vin killed the engine and turned to her slowly, showing her his hands.

"Look, the boss is going to be plenty steamed that we brought you to him. He actually likes coppers for the most part but…well, you're something different now, aren't you? If he hurts you or even kills you, this ain't going to be on my hands."

"Mine either," Tack said.

"I'll take my chances," Ava said. And though she thought it sounded confident, she could not deny that these comments had her suddenly wondering if this had been a massive mistake after all.

Ava got out first, as to keep an eye on her escorts. She was starting to feel more and more certain they weren't going to pose any threat, though. Now that they seemed content to take her to their boss—or "capo" as she'd started to learn from terminology back at the precinct—they almost seemed *willing* to be leading her along now.

When they came to the back door, Tack knocked heavily with the side of his fist. It was done in a pattern, almost like some sort of rhythm or beat so those inside would have no question about who was outside. The door was answered a few seconds later and the two men wasted no time entering.

Ava followed them inside and was instantly overwhelmed with the fragrant smells of Italian food. She smelled garlic, a thick tomato sauce, and what she thought might be a blend of spices that she could not identify. Vin and Tack led her down a thin hallway, and the man who had answered the door was ahead of them.

"Is he in?" Vin asked

"Yeah," the man in front said. "Who's the guest?"

"We'd rather not say just yet."

The man in front shrugged, as if he couldn't really care less. He then ventured off further down the hall and disappeared to the right, through a double set of swinging doors that Ava assumed led to the kitchen.

As for Vin and Tack, they came to a halt just outside of a door along the back hall. It was very basic, a wooden slab without glass or any sort of identifying sign. She noted that when Tack raised his hand to knock, he looked very nervous.

A voice instantly followed the knock. Ava was surprised at how cheerful and friendly it sounded. "Yeah? Come on in!"

Tack opened the door and entered. Vin followed, and Ava trailed in behind him as if she'd already been invited to do so. When she stepped into the room, she saw a man sitting behind a large and very cluttered desk. He was a little on the heavyset side and was dressed in a svelte suit. His hair was slicked back and a cigarette jutted from between his lips, sending little curls of smoke into the air.

He looked to Ava with a confused grin. Taking the cigarette out of his mouth and tapping ash into a large ashtray on the desk, he looked to Vin and Tack and asked, "Who's the dame?"

Ava did not let them answer for her. She took a bold step forward and answered for herself. "Ava Gold, detective with the NYPD."

The briefest little wave of concern crossed the man's face but it was quickly replaced by delight. "Ah, the lady detective the papers have all been talking about." He sat back in his chair and folded his arms over his chest. "And also the woman that took out three of my men last week, including taking Tony Two to jail for a while."

"Sir," Tack said timidly, "you can add two more men to that list. Billy and Dooley are still back at the dealership, knocked out cold."

"So I take it this isn't a friendly visit?" the man asked, looking to Ava.

She noticed that he had not revealed his name yet, and Vin nor Tack had bothered to give it. "Not exactly."

The office went silent for a moment before the man waved away Tack and Vin. "Get out of here," he said. "Thank you for escorting our visitor, but I think I'd like to have a private word with Detective Gold."

The two men obliged right away and headed for the door. Tack was the last to leave; he gave one final look into the office as if to make sure all was well, and then left. He closed the door gently behind him. When Ava was left in the room with this mysterious and seemingly powerful figure, she hated how anxious she became. She tried to imagine Frank in the same situation and wondered how he would respond. She then thought of Clarence in this same predicament and that seemed to calm her significantly.

"Is there something you have against my men, Detective Gold?" the man asked. He did not sound angry, but genuinely curious. "You seem to be targeting them."

"I'm targeting no one," she said. "No offense, but I don't even know your name."

He laughed at this, extinguishing his cigarette, and smiling up at her. "I forget just how new you are to the force. My name is August Bonnaci and I run a good portion of what you and your copper friends refer to as the mob. I also own this restaurant, and we make the meanest ravioli and stromboli in the whole damned city, if I do say so myself. Now, with introductions out of the way, tell me what grievance you have with me."

"You've read the papers. You know who I am and what I've done...including besting five of your men. I arrested Tony Two for suspicion of murder during the hatchet killer trial. And even though he ended up getting off, I've been harassed ever since. A gutted rat bleeding at my door. Someone breaking into my apartment through my window. I don't feel safe in my own home. I have a young son and a father that—"

"I assure you, these acts have not been approved by me. It could be Tony or one of his little thugs." He studied her for a moment and then added: "Is that truly the only reason you've come here?"

"Yes. I just need to know that my son is safe. And if that's a problem, I guess you know that I can make a fuss about it all. I can go to the papers. And let's face it...they seem to like me."

August chuckled; it was not as boisterous a laugh as his first one, and it unnerved Ava a bit. "I can see to it that the harassment stops. But first, I should tell you something. You're a cop, so I suppose you value the truth, yes?"

Ava only nodded, feeling that this was a trap of some kind.

"Right now, I have a pistol resting on my lap. I keep it holstered under my desk and whenever anyone knocks on my door, I take it down and place it on my lap. Currently, it is pointing directly at you and the bullets will tear right through the fake backing on my desk. The gun is a nice little number—a Ceska Zbrojovka I bought off of a local man that came home after the war. Do you believe me?"

"I do." The fear that she'd managed to keep mostly at bay grew stronger. She knew there was no way she could draw and then fire on him before he pulled off a few shots.

"Fortunately for you, I have no real interest in using it. You intrigue me, Detective Gold. You're clearly a great fighter and very smart...something I know *not* to be true of most other cops I've encountered. I'm also glad to see a woman getting this sort of opportunity and doing very well with it. That being said, here's what I will offer you—a trade, if you will. I will find out exactly who is harassing you in these ways and make them stop. But in return, you will owe me a favor."

Ava didn't waste much time thinking it over before she asked: "What's the favor?"

He laughed again, and the humor was back in it. He lit up another cigarette took a drag. "You really *are* quite new to this. The favor is not something I want now. But sometime in the future, I may need assistance of some kind from someone within the police. And when that time comes, I will call on you for the favor. You understand?"

"Yes," she said. She realized that she *had* fallen into a trap, though not the kind she'd been expecting.

"So we're agreed? I'll see that the harassment stops, and you'll owe me a favor later down the road."

"I'll agree, with a few conditions. I won't kill anyone, and I won't turn a blind eye to intentional murder."

August thought it over for a moment, mulling it behind a haze of cigarette smoke. "Yes, I think we can work with that. Detective Gold, we have a deal."

CHAPTER TWENTY SEVEN

Ava slept terribly that night at her father's apartment. She'd been disheartened when both Jeffrey and her father were both asleep when she got there and then lay awake trying to get a grip on what had happened with August Bonnaci. She understood that the mob now had a bit of power over her, but that was something she was willing to accept if it meant she could go to work knowing her family was safe. She was also plagued by the fact that while the Penny Pickett case would technically be considered closed, the wrong man would be going to jail for it—and it was mostly her fault.

In fact, Robert Abraham was the first person on her mind when she got out of bed. She was stirred awake by Jeffrey, getting dressed for the day. She looked to her son as he slipped a shirt on over his head. "Hey, buddy," she said. "I'm so sorry I got home so late last night."

"It's okay," he said, coming to sit next to her. "Grandpa said you were probably out late because you were chasing so many bad guys."

"I guess that was sort of true," she said. "Did Grandpa feed you?"

"Yeah. Sausage and grits. It was pretty good…but I don't like the way he makes his grits. They sort of taste like…I don't know. Like *rubber.*"

"Want to know a secret?"

"Yeah!"

She leaned in close to him and whispered: "I don't like the way he makes his grits, either."

They laughed a bit over this and then, over breakfast, Jeffrey told her all about what was going on at school. As she listened, something Jeffrey said resounded in her head. It had been a small comment, a comment meaning nothing when he'd said it, but it would not leave her head.

They sort of taste like…I don't know. Like rubber."

Like rubber. It made her think of the tire factory, the rubber and other materials at the Pickett tire plant. More than that, it made her think of people that, like Jeffrey having to eat those rubbery grits, might have been unhappy with working there. After all, she could not imagine George Pickett being an easy man to work for.

As she and Jeffrey spoke and she worked her way through this new, blossoming theory, Ava noted that her dad was nowhere to be found. She assumed he'd gone down to the gym early. She saw that this was indeed the case when she left to take Jeffrey to school. Her father was already working with an older-looking boxer at the rear of the gym, working over the punching bags. He saw them, gave a wave, and then his attention went back to the boxer. The fact that he'd not come over to speak made her think he was upset with her for her late night.

In other words, there was just one more thing to add to the maddening storm that was her life. She tried to keep it all buried as she walked Jeffrey to school She was pleased that he seemed to like it better now. She'd originally been afraid that the boy would shut down socially after his father died but it seemed like he was already managing to stay on track, especially at school.

After dropping Jeffrey off, she hurried for the precinct. She wondered if there was any way anyone at work had heard about her interactions with the mob last night. She could only assume that someone like August Bonnaci would keep such news close to his chest so he'd be able to call that favor in later down the road. There was a certain confidence in this, but it was still heavy on her mind as she arrived at the precinct. She headed to Frank's station at the rear of the bullpen right away. It was her hope that she might be able to talk Frank into helping her dig a bit deeper into the Pickett case. Sure, it was going to be considered closed a bit later today, but she was pretty sure even Frank suspected that Robert Abraham was not their man.

She found that as she neared his desk, she was a little excited about the idea. Maybe she was jazzed up from her fighting last night, or that she'd come face to face with August and not only left alive, but with a strange and tenuous partnership between them. Whatever it was, Ava felt like she could chew bullets and spit out nails as she approached Frank. The feeling seemed to come out of nowhere but was highly preferrable to the weight of everything she'd felt upon her when she'd come awake that morning.

"You look spry this morning," Frank told her as she approached.

"*Spry?*"

"You know…in a good mood. Sort of beaming, if that makes sense."

"I get what you mean but no, it doesn't make sense. If I'm looking *spry* about anything, it's just because I'm determined to prove that Robert Abraham is innocent."

"Well, the arrest was made official last night. So I don't see Minard going along with that suggestion."

"That's why we won't tell him. We can dig around and look for things that we might *accidentally* happen to stumble upon."

He looked irritated but she knew she had him. There was enough doubt in his own mind that he couldn't help but go along. "You'd think we would have accidentally stumbled upon those things during the investigation."

"Yes, maybe. But think about this: both George Pickett and Mack Duvall would have had much to gain from that wedding, right? But even now, before that wedding, they were fat cats with nice, cozy lives. And they shared one thing in common, right?"

"The plants and factories," Frank said.

"All that rubber," she said, recalling the innocent remark Jeffrey had made that had sparked the idea.

"What about it?"

"You saw the conditions there, right? Not terrible, but not the best by any means. And can you imagine trying to work for a man like George Pickett—a man that works his employees hard yet he's rarely there. Surely, somewhere along the line, he angered someone, right?"

"So now you're thinking an employee?"

"I think it's worth looking into. It fits with our theory that the killer was someone from outside of their social circle." She studied him and saw that he was having a very hard time coming to terms with it. Before he could argue at all, she forged on. "I'm going to check into it no matter what. I'd like it if you helped, but I don't expect you to."

He was looking at her in a way that took her off guard. It was more than just a way of studying her to gauge her sincerity. It was something else, something deeper. There was a softness there and it made her flush with a very quick heat.

"I'll go," he finally said. "But if we're caught somehow, I'll blame you. I'll say I figured out what you were up to and came to stop you. I'm sorry, but I can't lose my job for you."

Deal," she said.

Seems I'm making all kinds of deals as of late, she thought.

"Well, let's go ahead and get it over with, then," Frank said, getting up from his chair and grabbing his badge. "And in the meantime, you might want to think of some reason you would have been led back to the factory. Because even if this pans out for the good, that's one of the first things Minard is going to ask you about."

Ava had already started thinking about this and though she had no real answer just yet, she thought one might come to her before all was said and done.

Besides, it made no sense to her to have an answer for that if she had no real idea if this last-minute theory was going to pay off.

***

It was clear that a new shift had come on by simply looking at the workers. They weren't yet covered in filth, no one was sweating heavily yet, and most of the men out on the floor and behind the machines seemed to be in decent moods. The floors were also much cleaner than they had been during Ava and Frank's first visit.

After being ushered to the factory floor by a very nervous receptionist, Ava spotted the same foreman they'd spoken with during their first visit. Cal Nettle was walking around on the floor with a clipboard, stopping by each machine and asking the operator a quick question. He'd then scribble something down on a form on the clipboard. Ava and Frank approached him as he made his circuit between two machines. When he saw them coming, all of the color seemed to drain out of his face.

"Mr. Nettle," Ava said. "I was wondering if we could—"

"No," he said, waving his hands as if swatting away flies. "I can't speak with you. I've been given very specific instructions not to speak to the two of you."

"By George Pickett?" Frank asked.

"Yes. And that's all I can say." He then looked around quickly, a bit nervously in fact, and added: "I want to help. I really do. But I can't risk losing this job."

Ava understood this. Jobs like this one weren't easy to come by. Yet as she looked around at the other employees on the floor, an idea occurred to her. "Do you know if that same instruction was given to everyone else?"

A knowing and almost pleased look came to Nettle's face. "Not sure," he said. Then, with a shrug, he walked away staring at his clipboard.

"You really think anyone working here is going to be of any help?" Frank asked. "I'm certain Pickett has struck the fear of God into them."

"I go back to my earlier statement. A place like this, at least one person is going to have beef with him. We just need to ask—"

She stopped when she noticed something about the majority of the workers. She estimated that there were thirty or so men on the floor, either behind the machines, running the belts, or loading and unloading rubber. They all had their sleeves rolled up and the ones loading and unloading the machines were also wearing gloves. More specifically, the men running and unloading the machines seemed to have something streaked on their arms. It was brown in color with no distinct pattern, just smears of it here and there. It looked almost wet, but stuck to them like…

Like grease, Ava thought.

"Frank…look at their forearms."

"What?" But as soon as he'd asked the question, he seemed to see the same thing. If he said anything to her, Ava didn't hear it. She'd already started walking towards one of the men that had just unloaded a strip of rubber from the belt. He had added it to a small cart with a few other strips and started to push it along to the other side of the factory.

"Sir? Sir, excuse me," Ava said, rushing up to him.

"Yeah?" he asked, clearly irritated that he was being interrupted.

"What's that on your arms?"

"My arms?" He looked at them and then, seeing the grease, rolled his eyes at her and started walking again. Over his shoulder, he called out: "It's lubricant from the belt."

Ava walked to the nearest machine and saw the area where the belt came out of the back. It chugged along loudly and she could clearly see the lubricant on the underside of the belt. From what she could tell, it was used to make sure the wheels and rods continued to churn along. There was some of the lubricant on the concrete floor. Seeing it there brought it all home for her. She knelt down to look at it just as Frank joined her.

She looked up to him and said, "Look familiar?"

"Damned if it doesn't."

Just as Frank knelt down to get a better look, a loud male voice shouted from beside them. "Hey, who the hell are you two?"

They both stood, and Frank was quick to pull out his badge. "Detectives Wimbly and Gold, NYPD. This grease on the floor…it's used to lubricate the bearings and wheels for the belt, right?"

"Yes, sir," the employee said. His tone had changed drastically when he realized he was speaking to the police.

"And does it usually get all over the place like this?"

"Sometimes."

"How much do you use in any given shift?" Ava asked.

"I'm not too sure. I don't mess with it all that often. But I'd guess at least half a bucket or so."

Ava figured any questions they asked employees should be brief and to the point. The last thing she wanted was to draw more attention to themselves. She let her mind make the leaps and stretches it wanted, landing on a question she felt might help to lead them in the right direction.

"Sir, do you know if there have been any injuries on site as of late?"

He seemed to think about it for a moment, but it was clear he was nervous about it. "Gee, I honestly don't know. You should check with the people in the filing room."

"And where's that?" Frank asked.

The man, already starting to walk away from them, pointed behind them and to the left. Ava followed the direction of his finger and saw an office space above the factory floor, built in the far wall and accessible by a set of thick, wooden stairs. Ava started walking and as Frank followed, he asked a question that she pretty much expected.

"Injuries? How'd you get there?"

"I was trying to think of what sort of working conditions might drive someone to murder Penny. Firing, sure. That could be it. But I figure in an operation like this, if you get injured and have to miss work, you're probably replaced pretty quickly. So I went to the most extreme. And if we find nothing there, maybe then we settle on typical firings."

"Damn good thinking, Gold."

She did her best to not let the compliment go to her head as they reached the stairs. When they came to the top, there was a single door. It was closed but unlocked, so they let themselves inside. There were two large desks in a modest-sized room. A series of filing cabinets sat against the far wall, and an electric fan was plugged in, pointed at a tall, thin man sitting behind one of the desks. He wore wire-framed glasses and was currently hunched over a stack of paperwork. A beast of a typewriter sat beside him, a form currently rolled into it.

He looked to them and just as a question formed on his thin lips, Frank showed his badge. "Detectives Wimbly and Gold," he said. "We need to look at your recent injury reports. Where would we find them?"

The man behind the desk looked flabbergasted. "I don't…well, I don't think you can do that. I need to get Mr. Pickett's permission for that and as you know, he's dealing with—"

"Exactly," Ava said. "We know what he's dealing with. So, it's probably going to make him very angry if we have to bother him today for that permission. You either give us five minutes to check right now, or we'll go ask him for permission, telling him it's your fault that we had to bother him."

'Fine," the man hissed, though it was clear the idea of Ava's scenario terrified him. "Injury reports are in the bottom drawer in the second cabinet."

Ava walked to the cabinet and opened the bottom drawer. The folders and documents inside were immaculately organized, making it easy to find what they were looking for. Ava started three months back, taking out the stack of folders and placing them on the vacant desk. The stack wasn't very big at all; when she separated them out, they found only six reports.

They looked through them one by one. The first one Ava read concerned a man that broke three fingers on his right hand when they were bent too far back when a crate fell from the top of a stack and he tried to catch it. The second was, ironically, a man that slipped in a streak of belt lubricant and twisted his ankle. In both cases, the report made it quite clear that each accident was the fault of the worker, not the factory or the working conditions. Ava was opening up her third folder when she heard Frank utter a curse from beside her.

"Got something?" she asked.

"Yeah, I think so. Look at this."

He slid the folder over to her. The first thing she noticed was that it was several pages thicker than the two reports she'd already seen. She read over the report and within just two lines, she felt sure they had found something.

The report told the story of what was labelled "an irregular accident." Four employees had died in the space of about fifteen seconds when one of the belts on the machines snapped. From what the report said, the belt snapped because one of the rubber pressing machines threw a rod and malfunctioned. The report gave every scant evidence (likely intentional, if Ava had to guess) but even that brief glimpse was horrible enough.

The rod that was thrown tore through the side of the machine. It struck an employee in the back of the head, essentially crushing his skull. The thrown rod caused the belt to speed up and come untethered from the track. This increased the speed of the rubber strips coming off and one strip that was about a foot thick slammed into the chest of a worker at the end of the belt rail. This employee was thrown back into a cart which collided with a stack of crates, all filled with lubricant and various kinds of rubber. The crates fell over, some from a height of more than twelve feet, and fell on six people. Four survived with just scratches and, in one case, a broken arm. The other two, however died instantly.

Her own curse was lodged in her throat and nearly came out, but then she saw the most brutal fact of all. The employee that had been nailed by the flying chunk of rubber had only been thirteen years old. His name was Kevin Osmond, and his father was Steven Osmond…who just happened to be one of the employees that had survived the falling stack of crates.

Steven Osmond's injury report was part of the file. He'd suffered a deep cut on his left arm and nothing more. Meanwhile, his son had died either from having his chest crushed by the projectile from the machine, or from the falling crates.

Even more alarming was the fact that Steven Osmond's report came to an end with a single comment that sent a chill through Ava.

Steven Osmond had returned to work six weeks after his son's death. Based on what Ava could see, he was still an employee of Pickett Rubber.

"My God," she said, thumbing through the rest of the papers.

Frank, meanwhile, turned to the man behind the desk. "Is Steven Osmond currently working?"

"Osmond?" the tall, thin man asked. "No. He's night shift. You missed him by about an hour and a half."

Ava eyed the address listed for Steven Osmond and committed it to memory. As she put the file back into the cabinet, Frank was already at the door. It was another of those unspoken agreements: they both felt that Steven Osmond was the next logical stop.

And maybe even the final one.

CHAPTER TWENTY EIGHT

The address took them to the Five Points area in Harlem. Ava was not overly familiar with the area, though she had performed in a few clubs along some of the streets they passed by. It was only nine thirty in the morning, but something about the gloom of the streets made it feel like perpetual dusk. The difference between Harlem and the Fifth Avenue setting they'd been dealing with for the past two days was almost polarizing. It broke Ava's heart that a city that was supposed to be so full of promise and hope allowed people to live in two completely different states of life like this. It was also a stark picture of how men like George Pickett lived in excessive wealth because of the hard work of people that lived in places like these.

They came to the address twenty minutes after leaving the factory. Frank parked the car in a stretch of dirt in front of saltbox, ramshackle buildings. Ava noted outhouses behind a few of them, meaning there was no operational running water in this area just yet. After killing the engine, Frank moved to open his door but Ava stopped him.

"Maybe just me," she said. "Let me talk to him."

"Gold, he just got off of work and he lost a son not too long ago. This man is going to be a tired, emotional wreck."

"Exactly. The last thing he needs is two cops grilling him. He doesn't need some jacked up jobbie standing right in front of him, asking about his son's death."

His softened features told Ava that he saw her point. He sighed and said, "Okay. I'll give you five minutes."

"Ten. And trust me. If I get in any sort of trouble, I can defend myself."

"Oh, I know you can. Just….be careful."

She saw that softness in his eyes again and this time there was no doubt what it meant. Clarence had looked at her like that when they'd been courting. It was the absolute last thing she needed to see (or feel) from her partner before going in to speak with Steven Osmond. She got out of the car before it could get any stranger.

She felt Frank's eyes on her as she walked towards Steven's house. A series of old, wooden boards ran between the dirt lot and his low, dusty porch. There was no overhang, just a single platform a few inches off of the ground that led to his front door, which sat slightly crooked in its frame. She knocked on the thin, wooden door and then looked around to the dusty yards of the neighboring shacks. A few houses down, several African American children were playing with a ball in the dirt. On the other side of the dirt lot, two old men sat in small chairs, chatting idly about something.

She nearly knocked again, but the door was finally answered. There was no caution or hesitancy when it was answered. The door was opened completely, and Ava found herself looking at a man of about forty or so. There were dark bags under his eyes and Ava had no problem guessing this man may have not slept well in weeks. He was gaunt and unshaven, withered to a frail frame. In other words, the exact representation of someone that had recently lost a child but was still forced to work hard to make ends meet.

"Yeah?" the man, presumably Steven Osmond said. "Who are you?"

Before she answered, Ava noticed that there were slight brown smudges on his forearms and wrists. The poor man hadn't even showered from his shift yet. If he even had the easy accessibility to a shower, of course.

"Are you Steven Osmond?" Ava asked.

"I am. Who are you?" He considered this for a moment and shook his head. "Even in the morning, this place ain't fit for a lady."

She showed him her badge and introduced herself, doing her best to gauge his reaction. "I'm Detective Ava Gold, with the NYPD. My partner, Detective Frank Wimbly, is in the car behind us and over to the right a bit. I was wondering if I could have a word with you?"

He seemed to think about it for the briefest of moments but then gave a simple shrug and ushered her in. She stepped into his house and found it not only sweltering, but sparsely furnished. It was a simple two room set-up, with a single door off to the right that she assumed was a closet of some kind. The floor was made of cracked wood. She could see the dirt beneath the house between two of the boards. Two simple chairs occupied the main area, and a mattress without a frame sat in the second room, which was divided by only a wall and no door. There was no running water and the only light came from the windows and a small bulb hanging from a questionable socket in the center of the room.

"A lady detective, huh?" Steven said. "That's good. Glad to see it." He sat down in one of the chairs and looked at her with tired resignation.

"Can I be honest with you, Mr. Osmond?"

"Sure."

"You don't seem all that surprised that a detective was knocking at your door. Maybe a little shocked that it was a woman, but not a detective."

He shrugged and without taking his eyes from her, they started to well up with tears. "I figured someone was going to find out sooner or later."

She knew what was coming next. She could feel it in her heart, but she almost wanted this to come out to nothing. She wanted to be just as wrong about this as she had been about Robert Abraham. But her heart—as well as Steven Osmond's moist eyes—told her that was not going to be the case. Still, she had to hear him say it.

"Find out what, exactly?"

"I didn't leave fingerprints, did I? I was wearing my new work gloves. I'd just gotten them that day. Or was it maybe out on that damned ledge? I almost fell off of it. *Twice!* Oh, but I didn't care."

Ava decided to play along. She didn't think he was trying to be clever, to tell her everything but not give a confession. She just thought he needed some pushing.

"No. There was a smear of something on the floor. Something we now believe to be the lubricant used on the belts at the factory."

He nodded, frowning. "I guess, in a way, I'm happy someone knows. It's been eating at me and as soon as I left...I wish I hadn't done it. That girl didn't do nothing, you know? But because of her daddy, I lost..."

The tears streamed down his face now and he didn't bother wiping them away. He sobbed into his hands, and Ava again saw the grease on the back of his arms.

"I lost everything! If you know what I did, do you know *why?*"

"We do. We just found out about the accident...about Kevin."

Steven let out a roar at the sound of his son's name. It was such a guttural noise that Ava lifted her hand, placing it closer to her sidearm.

"Mr. Osmond, I need you to tell me what you did."

"You already know," he said, his voice still in something of a roar that was now muted by his tears. "You know."

Ava wanted to cry right along with him. He couldn't even bring himself to say what he'd done. "The factory labelled it an accident, I saw that," she said. "But I've also seen that factory, and I've spoken with Mr. Pickett a lot lately. Mr. Osmond, if you lost your son and—"

"I wanted him to feel it, too!" Steven suddenly screamed. "I wanted him to feel it, so I climbed up the back of the house, went across that ledge and found a way in. I...walked through that first room and came to his daughter's room. I didn't even think about it. all I saw was Kevin. When I took the life of his daughter, all I saw was my son and...and..."

He fell from the chair, sobbing. He drew in deep, hitching breaths and yelled into the dusty floor. "I'm so sick and tired...I'm so exhausted and I...I miss him so much!"

Ava gave him a moment, waiting for the tears to subside. She kept her voice low and felt a bit like a monster as she went about her job.

"Mr. Osmond, you have to come with me now. Do you understand that?"

He only nodded, still collecting his breath from the sobbing and screaming.

"Will you come easily, or am I going to have a problem with you?"

"No," he croaked. "No problem. I'm so tired. I can't sleep and...and I deserve it. I know I do. So, no. No problems out of me."

Ava nodded, doing her best not to cry in front of this man. Slowly, she walked to the door. "I'm going back to my car, Mr. Osmond. Take your time. I'll give you fifteen minutes and if you're not out by then, I'll come in with my partner next time."

"Yeah, okay." He then eyed her in a strange way and added: "Thank you."

It seemed like a strange thing to say, but it ushered Ava back out to the porch. She almost kept the door open, but she closed it, giving him his privacy. When she got back to the car, she realized that she *was* weeping a bit. She wiped a tear away from her cheek as she got back into the car.

"What's going on?" Frank asked. "Where is he?"

Looking to the house, Ava said, "He's coming. And he's not going to be a problem."

The door opened less than three minutes later. Ava watched Steven Osmond take a deep breath and then let it out with a shudder. He then walked slowly towards the car, his head hung low. Ava had to look away, scared that she might cry again.

He got into the back seat of the car and didn't say a single word all the way to the precinct.

CHAPTER TWENTY NINE

Later that day, Robert Abraham was released from his holding cell with nothing more than a missed gig. He was understandably bitter when he signed the paperwork for his release. Ava was standing at Frank's desk, waiting to speak with him as he made his way out, feeling that a sincere apology was the least she could offer him.

However, what she did not expect was the corresponding visit from George Pickett. At the same time Abraham was on his way across the precinct floor and back to his freedom (and, Ava hoped, many gigs to come) George entered the precinct. Ava only saw him because he came rushing past the welcome desk and to the precinct. He looked like a bull that had just been let out of the gates at a rodeo. When his eyes fell on Robert Abraham, he made a direct line straight to him.

"Ah hell," Ava said

Frank, who was speaking to another officer a few feet away, did not hear this. He also did not see it when Ava started walking quickly across the bullpen to cut Pickett off. Apparently, neither did George Pickett. His eyes were fixed on Robert Abraham and apparently, so was his mouth.

"You! What in the hell are you doing?" He then looked at the closest officers within earshot and addressed them. "This man killed my daughter and you're letting him go? Do you need *me* to dole out justice?"

He took a stride towards Abraham to do just that and when he did, Ava stepped between them. She held her hands out and gave him a gentle push. "No. This man is being released because we found Penny's killer. And he did not do it."

"And why should I believe you? You and your ignorant partner are why I'm here! I know you came to the plant today, and I know you looked in my files."

"We certainly did. And that's how we found your daughter's killer."

"You nosy bitch! Those files are none of your concern."

A few officers started to mill around, but did not dare say anything. Apparently, they were as spooked by Pickett's wealth as Minard appeared to have been at times. Frank was coming over, his face as pale as a sheet. Ava assumed it was because he feared she might end up doing something stupid.

Ava leaned closer to him and whispered: *"Nosy bitch* is an awfully strange way of saying *thank you."*

"Thank you? *Thank you?* I'm going to have your job before I leave here. I'll have your job and sue this entire precinct. You're nothing but—"

"I'd watch my mouth if I were you," Ava interrupted. "Your money doesn't blind everyone and in case you haven't noticed, you've got some pretty angry officers around you. This isn't Fifth Avenue, George. Here, you're the powerless one."

"Is that so?"

Frank appeared beside her. And then, to her horror and fascination, so did Captain Minard. He appeared out of nowhere, like a phantom.

"Yes," Minard said. "That is so. We have a suspect that has admitted to the murder of your daughter. He is going to be handed over to the courts and justice *will* be served."

Ava, unable to resist one final verbal jab, leaned in closer. "And unless you want copies of those injury reports to go public, I suggest you shut the hell up right now and get back to that fancy house of yours."

Now it was George Pickett that had gone ten shades of white. He looked at all of the cops surrounding him and started to walk backwards, unwilling to take his eyes off of them. "Yes, well…I'll just contact my lawyers about this."

But the words lacked power and emotion. George Pickett was scared out of his mind and was trying to find anything to say to make it seem otherwise.

Ava gave Minard a weary look as he headed back to his office. She wondered if Pickett *could* somehow disrupt or damage the department. Had Minard just put his neck out for her? She slowly made her way back over to Frank's desk. As she did, the precinct slowly resumed its normal volume. Back to normal, though, meant snide comments…some of which were a bit too loud to be covered up by the still-escalating noise.

"Crazy broad is going to think Pickett backed down to her," someone said nearby.

"She must be really buying into what those headlines are saying about her," someone else responded.

Ava paused for a moment and without much thought, turned to the left. She marched to the stairs that led down to the Women's Bureau and made her way into the office. The only familiar face she saw was Lottie. There were two others, but she could not recall their names. Ava did not say a word, even when Lottie gave her a bright and cheerful, "Hey, stranger!"

Ava looked on her old desk and thumbed through some of her old things. Among it all, she found the threatening note that had been left for her a few days ago after wrapping the hatchet-killer case. Without bothering to re-read it for the thousandth time, she yanked it up and headed back out of the WB office.

"Um, Ava, doll?" Lottie said. "Everything okay?"

"Maybe," was all she said as she headed back to the stairs.

She marched back upstairs and headed directly for Frank's desk with the letter still in her hand. "Frank, do you mind if I use your desk for a second?" she asked.

"Sure thing. What's going—"

Ava hefted one foot up onto the desk and then crawled onto it. She got to her feet and looked out over the offices and the bullpen. She had a momentary yet blinding moment of panic when everything in her body seemed to scream: *My God in Heaven, what are you DOING?* But that was quickly erased when, one by one, the officers and other employees of the precinct started to turn her way.

From below her, Frank inched closer to the desk. "Gold, would you *please* get down? What are you even doing?"

She ignored the question, and held the note up over her head. She then began to recite it from memory, speaking slowly and with authority.

"Congrats, Ava! Looks like you're going to do well with this job. It's a shame that women aren't meant to be cops. If you're still here in a month, I'm going to make things *so hard* for you. Have fun playing make believe while you can."

She looked down to all of them and saw that she had everyone's attention. The only moment of fear or panic she had was when she saw that Minard had also come to see what was going on. He stood at the entrance to his office, looking surprised and maybe even entertained. Ava continued, though, undaunted.

"Someone left this note on my desk about a week or so ago," she said. "Whoever did it is a coward because they did not sign it or leave a name. So I am going to take this moment to let the author of this note step away from his cowardice. I invite you to step out and face me like a man, right now, in front of your peers."

All of the officers below her looked around. Some looked angry while others just looked embarrassed over the entire situation. A few looked at the floor, just waiting for this awkward moment to come to an end.

"No? Fine. Then you'll remain a coward. And while I'm up here, I may as well take it a step further."

"Do you have to?" Frank whispered from just below her. He was perhaps more nervous and embarrassed than anyone else. But she also noticed that his eyes never left her.

"Now, I *am* a woman. I have breasts and I don't have that thing dangling between my legs that tends to make most of your decisions for you. So if there is anyone in this precinct that has a problem with me, a woman, being a detective, please say so now. Does anyone have a problem with me being a detective?"

There was silence for about two seconds. It was broken when someone near the center of the bullpen spoke up very loudly. "Hell yes, I have a problem with it." She identified him and. stared him down. He was an average-sized officer that looked to be pushing fifty. She thought his name was Truman or Tubman or something like that. "You have no business out on the streets with a badge," he continued. "It's bloody embarrassing for the NYPD. I didn't write the letter, but I should have. You need to resign and go home and be a mother to your kid. Take that advice to the bank. You'll thank me one day."

The remark about her son tore through her like lightning. "Maybe I'll just thank you now," she said as she hopped down from the desk.

She stormed across the bullpen, her glare basically daring someone to try to stop her. She approached Truman or Tubman or whatever the hell is name was and delivered a haymaker her father would have been proud of. It connected squarely, as the officer was so shocked by what was happening, he apparently didn't even think to block or try fighting back. He hit the floor hard and lay there, unmoving but groaning.

"Anybody else?" she asked, looking around the room. No one said a thing as she surveyed the room.

"No, no one else," Minard said from his place at his office door. "In fact, Gold, take the rest of the day. Get your things and take the rest of the day off. And then see me first thing tomorrow morning, in my office."

Ava nodded as she looked down to Truman or Tubman. She then walked to Frank's desk, where her badge and Steven Osmond's arrest reports sat. She gathered them up and looked back around to the still-staring precinct.

"Clarence would be ashamed of all of you," she said. "No one here seems interested in standing up for what is right. Clarence gave his life for you people—for this place. And this is how you all repay it? A threatening note? Silence when another detective is mocked?"

She'd had enough and, quite honestly, was afraid she'd say something she'd later regret if she kept going. She did say one thing as she picked up her things and started for the door, though. She turned to Frank and eyed him with as much sincerity as she could. She spoke softly, so only he would hear her.

"And you," she said, searching his eyes. "*You* are going to take me to dinner tomorrow night."

Frank was so shocked by the comment that he didn't have a chance to hide his smile. "Yes ma'am," she said, giving her a little nod.

Ava finally took her leave, realizing that she was leaving a bit of a wave behind her. The question remained, though, what that wave might dredge up. Would it bring change with it, or more of the same old tide, in and out, crashing on deaf ears?

***

It was good to be back at home, in her own apartment. More than that, it was good to meet Jeffrey as he came out of school and to let him know they'd be going back home—to their *actual* home. She and Jeffrey spent some time at the corner grocer's that afternoon, picking out things for dinner. Ever since she'd stepped foot in August Bonnaci's restaurant last night, she'd been craving something Italian. She'd only ever cooked an Italian dish once before and it had been a very basic spaghetti. So that afternoon, as they waited for her father to arrive from work, she and Jeffrey made a spaghetti sauce from scratch. It took some trial and error, but by the time Roosevelt was home from the gym, she had what she thought was a very passable sauce.

They ate and joked, and despite the day's events, Ava felt much more relaxed than she had the last time she'd had a meal in her apartment. She was sure she hadn't made any new friends with her little explosion and display at the precinct today, but it needed to be done and she did not regret it.

After dinner, as Jeffrey showered, she sat in the kitchen and spoke with her father over coffee. He eyed her with an amused sort of skepticism from over his cup. "So things are better now?"

"What do you mean?"

"Whatever problem you had that made you lower yourself to staying at my place. It's all wrapped up now?"

She thought of August Bonnaci and nodded. She was coming to understand that, in a roundabout way, she maybe had some form of mob protection at this point. She had no idea what sort of favor he might eventually ask of her, but she couldn't help but think he'd be keeping an eye out for such an asset; a cop that owed you a legitimate favor had to be a pretty great tool to have in your arsenal.

"Yes, I think everything is good. For now, I think they might even be better than good."

"I'm glad to hear it. It was nice to have you at my place, but let's face it…it's no place for a single mother to raise a boy."

"Speaking of which, please remember that you're welcome to stay here for a long period of time. As long as you want, actually."

"I don't know, Ava. I mean, I appreciate it and all, but—"

He stopped when a soft but noticeable sound reached their ears. It had sounded like a fluttering noise, almost like a bird had suddenly appeared in the apartment. Ava turned in the direction of the sound and saw that a sheet of paper had been slid beneath her door. She wondered if this might be from August, if he had already decided to cash in on that favor.

But when she picked it up, she found something altogether different. Something altogether unexpected.

It was a very brief letter, typed out. She read it to herself, holding the paper close.

"Ava, what is it?" Roosevelt asked.

She read it again before showing her father, wanting to make sure she'd read it correctly. The letter read:

Until today, I didn't know how strong you were. Clarence would be proud. I have some information about the man that killed him. I want to see this man brought to justice. But I'm going to need help, and it's something I want to cut you in on. I was a friend of Clarence's and, if you'll allow it, I'd like to be a friend of yours, too.

The letter had no name, which seemed odd. She slowly passed it over to her father, trying to figure out why someone would offer such information without giving a name.

For the moment, though, she didn't think a name was important. For now, what was important was that she knew she had a friend. A nameless friend, but a friend all the same.

And if the last few weeks were any indication, she was going to need every friend she could get.

CITY OF BONES
(An Ava Gold Mystery—Book 3)

When Ava Gold, New York City's first female detective, is called in to investigate the murder of a young woman beneath the Brooklyn Bridge, she quickly realizes this is no typical murder—and that she is up against no typical serial killer. To find him, her search will lead her into the rough streets and docks of burgeoning 1920s Brooklyn.

"A MASTERPIECE OF THRILLER AND MYSTERY. Blake Pierce did a magnificent job developing characters with a psychological side so well described that we feel inside their minds, follow their fears and cheer for their success. Full of twists, this book will keep you awake until the turn of the last page."
--Books and Movie Reviews, Roberto Mattos (re Once Gone)

CITY OF BONES (An Ava Gold Mystery—Book 3) is a new novel in a long-anticipated new series by #1 bestseller and USA Today bestselling author Blake Pierce, whose bestseller Once Gone (a free download) has received over 1,000 five star reviews.

In the rough streets of 1920s New York City, 34 year-old Ava Gold, a widower and single mom, claws her way up to become the first female homicide detective in her NYPD precinct. She is as tough as they come, and willing to hold her own in a man's world.

But Ava, facing resentment and opposition from her all-male police force, has been transferred to a downtown precinct, and hazed relentlessly in the hope that she will become miserable enough to drop out.

Ava, pushed to the edge, will have to rely on her brilliant intellect to enter the killer's mind, to prove herself, and to stop him before he strikes again.

A heart-pounding suspense thriller filled with shocking twists, the authentic and atmospheric AVA GOLD MYSTERY SERIES is a riveting page-turner, endearing us to a strong and brilliant character that will capture your heart and keep you reading late into the night.

Books #4-#6 are also available!

Blake Pierce

Blake Pierce is the USA Today bestselling author of the RILEY PAGE mystery series, which includes seventeen books. Blake Pierce is also the author of the MACKENZIE WHITE mystery series, comprising fourteen books; of the AVERY BLACK mystery series, comprising six books; of the KERI LOCKE mystery series, comprising five books; of the MAKING OF RILEY PAIGE mystery series, comprising six books; of the KATE WISE mystery series, comprising seven books; of the CHLOE FINE psychological suspense mystery, comprising six books; of the JESSE HUNT psychological suspense thriller series, comprising nineteen books; of the AU PAIR psychological suspense thriller series, comprising three books; of the ZOE PRIME mystery series, comprising six books; of the ADELE SHARP mystery series, comprising thirteen books, of the EUROPEAN VOYAGE cozy mystery series, comprising four books; of the new LAURA FROST FBI suspense thriller, comprising six books (and counting); of the new ELLA DARK FBI suspense thriller, comprising nine books (and counting); of the A YEAR IN EUROPE cozy mystery series, comprising nine books, of the AVA GOLD mystery series, comprising six books (and counting); and of the RACHEL GIFT mystery series, comprising six books (and counting).

An avid reader and lifelong fan of the mystery and thriller genres, Blake loves to hear from you, so please feel free to visit www.blakepierceauthor.com to learn more and stay in touch.

BOOKS BY BLAKE PIERCE

RACHEL GIFT MYSTERY SERIES
HER LAST WISH (Book #1)
HER LAST CHANCE (Book #2)
HER LAST HOPE (Book #3)
HER LAST FEAR (Book #4)
HER LAST CHOICE (Book #5)
HER LAST BREATH (Book #6)

AVA GOLD MYSTERY SERIES
CITY OF PREY (Book #1)
CITY OF FEAR (Book #2)
CITY OF BONES (Book #3)
CITY OF GHOSTS (Book #4)
CITY OF DEATH (Book #5)
CITY OF VICE (Book #6)

A YEAR IN EUROPE
A MURDER IN PARIS (Book #1)
DEATH IN FLORENCE (Book #2)
VENGEANCE IN VIENNA (Book #3)
A FATALITY IN SPAIN (Book #4)

ELLA DARK FBI SUSPENSE THRILLER
GIRL, ALONE (Book #1)
GIRL, TAKEN (Book #2)
GIRL, HUNTED (Book #3)
GIRL, SILENCED (Book #4)
GIRL, VANISHED (Book 5)
GIRL ERASED (Book #6)
GIRL, FORSAKEN (Book #7)
GIRL, TRAPPED (Book #8)
GIRL, EXPENDABLE (Book #9)

LAURA FROST FBI SUSPENSE THRILLER
ALREADY GONE (Book #1)
ALREADY SEEN (Book #2)
ALREADY TRAPPED (Book #3)
ALREADY MISSING (Book #4)

ALREADY DEAD (Book #5)
ALREADY TAKEN (Book #6)

EUROPEAN VOYAGE COZY MYSTERY SERIES
MURDER (AND BAKLAVA) (Book #1)
DEATH (AND APPLE STRUDEL) (Book #2)
CRIME (AND LAGER) (Book #3)
MISFORTUNE (AND GOUDA) (Book #4)
CALAMITY (AND A DANISH) (Book #5)
MAYHEM (AND HERRING) (Book #6)

ADELE SHARP MYSTERY SERIES
LEFT TO DIE (Book #1)
LEFT TO RUN (Book #2)
LEFT TO HIDE (Book #3)
LEFT TO KILL (Book #4)
LEFT TO MURDER (Book #5)
LEFT TO ENVY (Book #6)
LEFT TO LAPSE (Book #7)
LEFT TO VANISH (Book #8)
LEFT TO HUNT (Book #9)
LEFT TO FEAR (Book #10)
LEFT TO PREY (Book #11)
LEFT TO LURE (Book #12)
LEFT TO CRAVE (Book #13)

THE AU PAIR SERIES
ALMOST GONE (Book#1)
ALMOST LOST (Book #2)
ALMOST DEAD (Book #3)

ZOE PRIME MYSTERY SERIES
FACE OF DEATH (Book#1)
FACE OF MURDER (Book #2)
FACE OF FEAR (Book #3)
FACE OF MADNESS (Book #4)
FACE OF FURY (Book #5)
FACE OF DARKNESS (Book #6)

A JESSIE HUNT PSYCHOLOGICAL SUSPENSE SERIES

LURING (Book #3)
TAKING (Book #4)
STALKING (Book #5)
KILLING (Book #6)

RILEY PAIGE MYSTERY SERIES
ONCE GONE (Book #1)
ONCE TAKEN (Book #2)
ONCE CRAVED (Book #3)
ONCE LURED (Book #4)
ONCE HUNTED (Book #5)
ONCE PINED (Book #6)
ONCE FORSAKEN (Book #7)
ONCE COLD (Book #8)
ONCE STALKED (Book #9)
ONCE LOST (Book #10)
ONCE BURIED (Book #11)
ONCE BOUND (Book #12)
ONCE TRAPPED (Book #13)
ONCE DORMANT (Book #14)
ONCE SHUNNED (Book #15)
ONCE MISSED (Book #16)
ONCE CHOSEN (Book #17)

MACKENZIE WHITE MYSTERY SERIES
BEFORE HE KILLS (Book #1)
BEFORE HE SEES (Book #2)
BEFORE HE COVETS (Book #3)
BEFORE HE TAKES (Book #4)
BEFORE HE NEEDS (Book #5)
BEFORE HE FEELS (Book #6)
BEFORE HE SINS (Book #7)
BEFORE HE HUNTS (Book #8)
BEFORE HE PREYS (Book #9)
BEFORE HE LONGS (Book #10)
BEFORE HE LAPSES (Book #11)
BEFORE HE ENVIES (Book #12)
BEFORE HE STALKS (Book #13)
BEFORE HE HARMS (Book #14)

AVERY BLACK MYSTERY SERIES
CAUSE TO KILL (Book #1)
CAUSE TO RUN (Book #2)
CAUSE TO HIDE (Book #3)
CAUSE TO FEAR (Book #4)
CAUSE TO SAVE (Book #5)
CAUSE TO DREAD (Book #6)

KERI LOCKE MYSTERY SERIES
A TRACE OF DEATH (Book #1)
A TRACE OF MURDER (Book #2)
A TRACE OF VICE (Book #3)
A TRACE OF CRIME (Book #4)
A TRACE OF HOPE (Book #5)